BOOKS BY
C. S. FORESTER

MR. MIDSHIPMAN HORNBLOWER

LIEUTENANT HORNBLOWER

HORNBLOWER AND THE ATROPOS

CAPTAIN HORATIO HORNBLOWER
(*consisting of* BEAT TO QUARTERS, SHIP OF THE LINE *and* FLYING COLOURS)

* COMMODORE HORNBLOWER

* LORD HORNBLOWER

* ADMIRAL HORNBLOWER IN THE WEST INDIES

HORNBLOWER AND THE HOTSPUR

THE INDOMITABLE HORNBLOWER
(*consisting of the three volumes starred above*)

THE HORNBLOWER COMPANION

HORNBLOWER DURING THE CRISIS

THE CAPTAIN FROM CONNECTICUT

THE SHIP

THE GOOD SHEPHERD

THE LAST NINE DAYS OF THE BISMARCK

POO-POO AND THE DRAGONS

POO-POO AND THE DRAGONS

POO-POO AND THE DRAGONS

By C. S. FORESTER
Illustrated by ROBERT LAWSON

BOSTON   LITTLE, BROWN AND COMPANY   TORONTO

LIBRARY OF CONGRESS CATALOG CARD NO. 42-17225

Second Printing

PRINTED IN THE UNITED STATES OF AMERICA

PREFACE

For Adults Only

IT ALL STARTED because the boy was moping for his mother. The odd thing was that I never thought of that explanation because he is usually so tough that I could not attribute to him such a weakness as to mope for a mother three thousand miles away. But the point was that for the first time in eight years of a misspent life he decided not to eat, and his worried father, tottering under his burden of responsibility, and with explanations to make sooner or later, remembered very acutely (and it did not lighten his burden) how all the books tell you not to coax in these circumstances. It was at the eleventh hour that Poo-Poo came to my rescue. At each mealtime I told the story of Poo-Poo's adventures with the simple proviso that the moment eating stopped, the story stopped, absolutely dead, and was not resumed until the next mouthful went in. It worked well enough, especially if I could manage to time things so that there was a denouement obvious in the immediate future, just at the moment when the first helping had been finished, and there was some doubt as to whether a second helping would be asked for.

vii

Of course there was the obvious corollary that as long as the eating went on the story had to go on, and long after the original cause for Poo-Poo had evaporated with the return of the boy's mother, Poo-Poo went on without any cause. It became a sort of competition between my powers of invention and the boy's capacity for food. I don't know of a stronger recommendation for my digestion (renowned through two continents as being better than an ostrich's) than that over a period of a good many months now I have spent about three quarters of my dinner-times inventing Poo-Poo and have not had dyspepsia yet. Fortunately I have had the sense, on the days when I suspected that the well of inspiration would be drying up, to sneak out quietly and have dinner in the tranquillity of a restaurant.

POO-POO AND THE DRAGONS

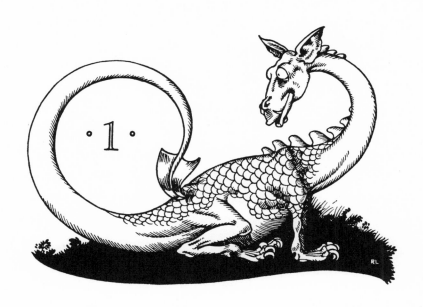

ONCE THERE WAS a boy called Poo-Poo. His other names were HAROLD HEAVYSIDE BROWN, and it might be just as well to remember them. On Saturday morning Poo-Poo (what were his other names?) was wondering what to do, because all his friends were doing something else. First he tried to play inside the house, but his mother (her name was MRS. BROWN) turned him out because she wanted to do the cleaning. Then he went to play at the back of the house, but his father (and his name was MR. BROWN and he was a VERY CLEVER MAN) sent him away because, as he said, he did not feel like answering questions that morning, and then Poo-Poo (what were his other names?) found himself in the front of the

3

house and wondering harder than ever what he should do. So he walked down the street a little way, and around the corner and along the road until he came to a vacant lot — which had a dragon on it.

He was a nice dragon, quite a fair size as dragons go, — something between a duck and a motor bus, — and he was running about in the long grass and swishing his tail and he looked rather like a dachshund who has been taking lessons from a polliwog, and he was not quite as brilliant as dragons sometimes are because he was only black and blue and purple and white and green and red and yellow and orange and violet and magenta with spots of other colors here and there.

The dragon was very pleased to see Poo-Poo (what were his other names?), and he came galloping up to him through the long grass and he skipped about and he swished his long tail and he shot out his long tongue, which would have looked like an eel if it had not looked like a slice of bacon, and he licked Poo-Poo's hand and then he galloped away and he came back and licked Poo-Poo's legs so that they tickled and he ran round in circles and he was a very friendly dragon indeed. So Poo-Poo patted him behind the ears and tried to stroke his back and found it was too spiky and he went on across the field with the dragon galloping round him. And at the far side of the field there was a little wooden building with a sign over it and on the sign were the words: MAXWELL MURRAY McIN-TOSH, CHIMNEY POTS CONSTRUCTED.

Inside the building there was a man sitting in a chair making belts out of umbrella handles.

Now Poo-Poo was a very polite boy, so he went up to the man and said: "Excuse me."

And the man said, "Yes, I excuse you."

And Poo-Poo said, "Excuse me, Mr. McIntosh, but is this your dragon?"

And Mr. McIntosh said, "Now do I *look* like a man who has a dragon?"

And Poo-Poo said, "I've never seen anyone who did have a dragon."

"That's a very extraordinary thing," said Mr. McIntosh. "You can't have traveled very far."

"I think I'm going to, one of these days," said Poo-Poo.

"Well, I shan't stop you," said Mr. McIntosh. (Can you remember what Mr. McIntosh's first names were?)

"I should like to know the way home if you please," said Poo-Poo (remember he was always a very polite boy).

"Some think it's one way and some think it's the other," said Mr. McIntosh. "But the one thing to be sure of is that whichever way you go you'll think the other way was the right way. But go whichever way you like and you'll find that you'll come to another place."

"Thank you," said Poo-Poo, still being very polite and rubbing his leg where the dragon had licked it impatiently. "I'll try to remember that. Good morning." And Poo-Poo went on

5

across the field with the dragon skipping and galumphing, clippety-clop, round and round him.

And they came to a tremendous big ladder, and Poo-Poo started to climb it, and he had only got a little way up when the dragon came up the ladder with a tremendous rush after him and climbed straight onto Poo-Poo's shoulder, and then went on up the ladder in front of him.

Have you ever seen a dragon running up a ladder? It is one of the most surprising things you could see anywhere. He went up jumping, with all four feet at once, about six rungs at a time; and at every jump he made the ladder spring in and out and all the spines on his back went "rattle-rattle," and on the end of his tail there was a spike like a big arrowhead which shook in Poo-Poo's face every time the dragon made a jump, so that Poo-Poo had to hold on very tight to the ladder and shout up to the dragon: —

"Take your silly old tail out of my face and don't jump so much!"

Poo-Poo only had to say it once, and then the dragon coiled up his tail in a neat roll and walked up the ladder the way respectable dragons walk up a ladder, with Poo-Poo climbing up behind him and needing to puff a little bit as the ladder went on and on and on.

When they got to the top there was the end of a big iron pipe sticking out of the ground with a waterfall running into it. And the dragon drew his head in and made his neck very short

6

and held his legs up close to his body and put his tail down underneath him and all the way along to the front so that he could hold the spike in his mouth, and when he had made himself look as much like a length of pole as any dragon can look, he tucked the front end of himself into the pipe and the water pushed him on and Poo-Poo came on after him. So they went swish down the length of the pipe with the water foaming all around them and it was a very exciting experience until they came out splash into the lake at the end. The dragon twirled his tail round and round so that it made the finest propeller you ever saw, and he went across that lake like lightning so that Poo-Poo had to swim very hard to keep up with him.

And at the other side the dragon scrambled out and shook himself and swung his tail about so that he made Poo-Poo quite wet with all the water he shook off himself. And they went along the street a little way and up another path, and before Poo-Poo could think where he was they were at the back door of his house and he was wondering what his mother would say about the dragon.

But you will have to wait until tomorrow before you hear what Poo-Poo's mother did say.

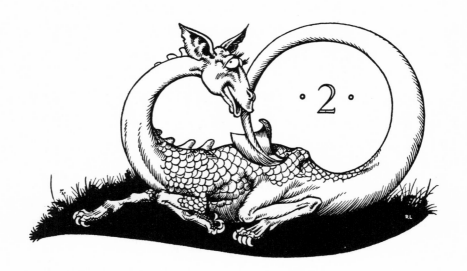

POO–POO'S MOTHER was in the kitchen beside the back door when Poo-Poo came in, and she said, "Oh, there you are," the way she often did say, and then she saw the dragon, and she said: —

"What have you brought that dragon home for?"

And Poo-Poo said, "I like him," and the dragon wagged his tail and squirmed and wriggled and started coming in through the door.

Poo-Poo's mother said: "We don't want dragons in this house."

And Poo-Poo said: "But he's a very nice dragon."

And Poo-Poo's mother said, "All the same, I don't want him in this house."

8

Then Poo-Poo's father came out, and he stopped and looked at the dragon as he squirmed and wriggled halfway through the door.

"Poo-Poo's brought a dragon home with him," said Poo-Poo's mother.

"That's what it looks like," said Poo-Poo's father. "Where did you find him, son?"

"He was on a vacant lot beside the house of the man who mends chimney pots," said Poo-Poo, "Mr. —— Mr. ——"

But Poo-Poo could not remember the name of the man who constructed chimney pots. I wonder if you can.

"Well," said Poo-Poo's father, "I think you'd better take him back where he came from."

"Oh," said Poo-Poo disappointed, "but I don't think he could possibly get up the pipe."

"Up the pipe?" said Poo-Poo's father.

"Well that was the way we came," said Poo-Poo.

This time it was Poo-Poo's father who said "Oh!" And he felt in his pockets and brought out a cigarette and then he began to look for a match, and he felt first in his trouser pockets and then in his coat pockets and then he began to look around the room, and as he did that the dragon opened his mouth with a click like a cigarette lighter and a long flame came out of his mouth the way it does with dragons.

"That's very convenient," said Poo-Poo's father, lighting his cigarette.

9

And the dragon shut his mouth and put the flame out and wagged his tail with pleasure.

"There — you see?" said Poo-Poo. "Can't I keep him?"

"Not if your mother — " said Poo-Poo's father — "And don't you expect me to go into any argument about it because I've got all that lawn to mow, and I'm not in a fit state to argue."

And then Poo-Poo's father looked out of the kitchen window and he stopped suddenly and he took his cigarette out of his mouth and he said, "My golly!" And Poo-Poo's mother looked out of the window and Poo-Poo peeked round the door, and they saw that the dragon's long wriggling tail had mowed that lawn as close as a billiard table.

"Now there's something to be said for a dragon that can mow lawns," said Poo-Poo's father looking at Poo-Poo's mother. "I've always said I'd rather go to the dentist three times a week than mow lawns."

"But all the same we don't want any dragons here," said Poo-Poo's mother. "He'd only mean a lot of work and bother."

And while she said this the front half of the dragon that was in the kitchen door went on squirming and wriggling first this way and then the other.

"You see," said Poo-Poo's mother, "I just couldn't have a dragon in the house who did that."

But then she looked and she saw that the floor that the dragon had been wriggling on was polished up by the dragon's wriggles so brightly that you could see your face in it without stooping.

"Well," said Poo-Poo's mother, "that's very nice, but — "

"I'm sure he'll work very hard," said Poo-Poo. "Please let me keep him."

"Oh, very well," said Poo-Poo's mother.

And Poo-Poo began to jump about the floor and the dragon began to wriggle harder than ever until Poo-Poo's mother had to say, "Now stop it, this minute!"

"What shall we call him?" asked Poo-Poo.

"Well," said Poo-Poo's father (do you remember that he was a very clever man?), "he looks as if his name was HORATIO."

And he had no sooner said the name when the dragon nodded and smiled and was just going to start wriggling all over again, when he remembered Poo-Poo's mother and left off hurriedly.

"Yes," said Poo-Poo's father, "that's it. HORATIO HEAVY–SIDE DRAGON. It's quite a good name."

(If I were you I should try to remember what the dragon's name is.)

"It's dinnertime," said Poo-Poo's mother, "and I don't know what dragons eat."

But of course Poo-Poo's father knew what dragons had for dinner.

"Oh — this and that," said Poo-Poo's father. "On Tuesdays they have to have the other thing, and on Fridays they have to have something else; and on Sundays, it's just as well to give them something different; and you must think up something new for Mondays and Wednesdays. On Saturdays it doesn't matter much, and on Thursdays they'll eat anything that's going."

"Well, that's all right then," said Poo-Poo's mother. "We'd better have dinner right away."

So they had dinner, and the dragon ate first one thing and then the other, and he had a second helping of something else, and he finished up with whatever there was, and his manners were as good as gold as he sat on the floor with his chin on the table and his tail stretching out through the door out into the street. And every time they called him Horatio (I hope you remember what his other names were) he nodded and smiled. Whenever Poo-Poo's father made a joke he laughed politely, and whenever Poo-Poo's mother wanted anything out of the kitchen he turned his head around and shot out his long neck and brought it in quicker than lightning.

NOW MR. BROWN had a rule about Poo-Poo going to the movies. He did not think that Poo-Poo should go there very often, and so the rule was that Poo-Poo could go on the fifth Saturday of every month as long as it fell on a Friday. But today Mr. Brown said that as it had very nearly happened because Friday was only one day back, they could all go to the movies that afternoon. So Poo-Poo and Mr. Brown and Poo-Poo's mother all got into the car and drove down the hill with the dragon going clippety-clop after them and Poo-Poo looking out of the window and waving to him, and Poo-Poo's father parked the car and they walked across to the theater and Mr. Brown bought three tickets.

13

"And what about that dragon?" said the lady at the window. (Her name was AMELIA MONTGOMERY.)

"I won't have to pay for him," said Mr. Brown, "because he won't be occupying a seat."

"I don't know about that," said the lady at the window (what was her name?), "he'll be going inside the theater, won't he?"

"But you don't charge for dragons," said Mr. Brown, "anyone can see that."

And he pointed to the notice which said MATINEE PRICES.

"You've got a charge for adults," said Mr. Brown, "and you've got a charge for children, and because you don't say anything about dragons it's obvious that you don't make any charge for them."

"I hadn't looked at it that way," said the lady at the window (I expect you have forgotten her name already). "But that doesn't mean to say that we'd let dragons in."

"Oh yes it does," said Poo-Poo's father, still pointing at the notice. "You say, 'The Management reserves the right to refuse admission to any person for any reason whatever,' but a dragon isn't a person, and so you can't refuse him admission, now can you?"

By this time there were a lot of people waiting behind Mr. Brown to buy tickets, so Miss Amelia Montgomery said, "Oh, very well then," just like Poo-Poo's mother sometimes. And they went along into the theater. Poo-Poo and his father and mother sat down in the seat and Horatio stretched himself out

14

along the aisle with his head beside Poo-Poo's knee, and Horatio was very good indeed and did not mind at all even when people fell over him in the darkness. Very soon the picture began.

Poo-Poo enjoyed the picture very much and was very excited when the cowboys started riding off after the rustlers; but then some Indians came on the screen and Poo-Poo's father (you know what his name was by now, but you must never forget that he was a very clever man) sat up and became very nervous.

"There may be trouble," said Poo-Poo's father. "Dragons don't like Indians. There's been a feud between them since Columbus discovered America. Horatio, be quiet."

He said it just in time for this once, because Horatio was already sitting up and moving restlessly about in the aisle when Poo-Poo's father spoke to him. He sat down again, but it could not last very long because very soon the Indians brought out their guns. He got up, and before Poo-Poo's father could stop him again he made one jump and went straight through the screen!

"My golly," said Poo-Poo's father. "There's going to be trouble about this."

And the lady beside him (she was called ARAMINTA WIGGINS) said very crossly: "People who bring dragons to the movies ought to keep them under proper control."

So Poo-Poo's father (you have heard that Poo-Poo was very polite, and that was because his father was, as well as being a very clever man) said, "I'm very sorry, madam."

15

What with Horatio being half through the screen and his tail waving about outside it, nobody in the theater could see anything of the picture at all, and there were a great many other complaints as well as from the lady sitting beside Mr. Brown (I expect you've forgotten her name already), and Mr. Brown stood up and said: —

"It looks to me as if we had better get out of this, *quick*."

So they stood up with Poo-Poo very excited, and Poo-Poo said, "Come along, Horatio!" — and they scuttled out of one of the side doors as quick as they could and ran across the road, and Poo-Poo and his father and mother jumped into the car and Poo-Poo's father drove like mad up the hill, so fast that Horatio, instead of going clippety-clop behind them, was going clippety-*clippety*-clop, and sometimes even clippety-*clippety-clippety*-clop. They got home, and they had hardly put the car into the garage when they heard the police sirens coming up the hill.

"There, you see?" said Poo-Poo's father. "They're after us already."

"Will they do anything to Horatio?" asked Poo-Poo.

"They'll want to put him in prison, I expect," said Mr. Brown, "and we can't have that, can we?"

"Oh, no, we can't," said Poo-Poo's mother, and Horatio laid his nose on the ground and looked very frightened indeed.

"We'll have to hide him," said Poo-Poo's father. He looked

16

round him and went on, "But it's not going to be so easy to hide a dragon around here."

Of course Poo-Poo's father had a good idea. Beside the road outside the garage there was a long drain for carrying off storm water, and Mr. Brown said, "Here, Horatio, make yourself as small as you can and crawl up there."

So Horatio made himself as small as he could and wriggled up the drain, but when he was in it his nose still stuck out at one end while his tail stuck out at the other.

"Can't you make yourself smaller than that?" said Poo-Poo's father. But when Horatio tried, the drain bulged up in the middle and Poo-Poo's father had to tell him to stop, while the noise of the siren was getting nearer and nearer.

"Quick," said Poo-Poo's father to Poo-Poo. "Sit on Horatio's nose and you, my dear, please sit on his tail."

So Poo-Poo sat on Horatio's nose and Mrs. Brown sat on Horatio's tail, just in time as the policeman on his motorcycle came round the corner and stopped.

"I'm looking for a dragon," said the policeman (his name was PATRICK MACGILLICUDDY).

"That's very interesting," said Poo-Poo's father.

"I want to arrest him," said the policeman (if you can't remember what his name was it isn't much use going on with the story), "for malicious damage to property."

"That's more interesting than ever," said Poo-Poo's father, "and it's very kind of you to tell us about it, but I don't see why you should."

17

"I have information," said Policeman Macgillicuddy, "that the dragon is domiciled here."

"Now look," said Poo-Poo's father, "can you see any dragons here?"

And the policeman (I hope you've remembered his name this time) looked round him and of course there were no dragons in sight at all.

"Perhaps you have been misinformed," said Poo-Poo's father; "what a pity that you have come all this way for nothing."

"I wonder why the lady and the little boy are sitting in the road like that?" asked the policeman.

"I can think of all sorts of possible reasons," said Poo-Poo's father (who was a very clever man); "perhaps they are sitting there because they think there are chairs there, although there aren't any; or perhaps their feet hurt them, or perhaps they're playing at trains, or perhaps they're waiting for someone to come along, or perhaps that's where they sit when they're not sitting anywhere else. Or perhaps their legs won't hold them up. Or perhaps it's because they like it."

"It might be something like that," agreed the policeman, a little bewildered.

"It's very nice talking to you like this," said Poo-Poo's father, "but I don't think I ought to keep you here when you have to go out and hunt for dragons. I wouldn't interfere with your doing your duty for anything. Good afternoon, Officer, and thank you very much for our very pleasant conversation."

"Good afternoon," said the policeman, more bewildered than ever. And he got on his motorcycle and went away.

"Now," said Poo-Poo's father to Horatio, "you can come out." And Horatio wriggled and he wriggled and he wriggled, and he couldn't manage to get another inch farther down the pipe.

"Come out backwards, then," said Poo-Poo, and Horatio wriggled and wriggled and wriggled and he couldn't manage to go backwards up the pipe either. He was stuck quite tight.

"My gracious," said Poo-Poo's mother. "What are we going to do now? Come along, Horatio, try again."

And Horatio wriggled and he wriggled and he wriggled but he was stuck quite tight.

"This is just terrible," said Poo-Poo's mother.

"Of course," said Poo-Poo's father (do you remember anything special about him?), "we don't have to worry very much because Horatio has only got to stay there with nothing to eat for a few days and then he'll be thin enough to come out again."

"But we don't want to do that," said Poo-Poo's mother.

"No, we don't want to do that at all," said Poo-Poo, and the dragon shook his head very mournfully and looked as if he were just going to cry.

"Can't you think of anything else?" asked Poo-Poo's mother, because she knew that Poo-Poo's father was a very clever man.

"Well, yes," said Poo-Poo's father. "Some people would use dynamite and some people would use pneumatic drills and some people would get a lot of men with spades to dig him out, and some people would dig a tunnel underneath, but all I want is just a feather. Poo-Poo, find me a feather."

So Poo-Poo found a feather and his father stooped down where the tip of Horatio's tail was sticking out of the pipe.

"It's a good thing," said Poo-Poo's father, "that dragons are very ticklish." He took hold of the spiky part shaped like an arrowhead at the end of Horatio's tail, and began to tickle Horatio on the joint just above it. And as he tickled Horatio began to squirm, and he squirmed and he wriggled more and more frantically and more and more frantically until at last there was a tremendous crash and the drainpipe split all the way along its length and Horatio came out through the top very pleased with himself.

"That isn't quite what I intended," said Poo-Poo's father, rather disappointed because the noise had been very loud indeed and now there was this great big long hole right across the road from one side to the other.

"It will take a very clever man to explain what has happened here," said Poo-Poo's father. (So you see that it was just as well that Poo-Poo's father was a very clever man.)

And he had no sooner said this than they heard the policeman's siren going again.

"Quick," said Poo-Poo's father to Poo-Poo's mother. "Take this dragon away. Take him away, I don't mind where you take him as long as he's out of sight quicker than lightning."

So Poo-Poo's mother ran up the garden with Horatio scuttling along behind her, and they had just got round the side of the house when up came the policeman (whose name of course you remember).

"My goodness gracious me," said the policeman, getting off his motorcycle, "whatever has happened here?"

"Well," said Poo-Poo's father, "of course it might have been an earthquake, or on the other hand it might be just a landslide. And then again some heavy truck might have come along the road and squashed it in, and there is always the possibility that it was rats. Or maybe some little boy was flying a kite in the next block and that made the pipe fall in."

"That doesn't sound very likely to me," said Policeman Macgillicuddy.

"It doesn't sound very likely to me either," said Poo-Poo's father. "But I was only trying to make a helpful suggestion."

"I think we'd better call it an earthquake," said the policeman, taking out his notebook and licking his pencil the way his mother always told him not to.

And so now you know the true history of the earthquake at Poo-Poo's house. All the newspaper reporters for a hundred miles round came to see that hole, and they asked Poo-Poo's father all sorts of questions, and the newsreel people brought their cameras and took a lot of photographs, and geologists came from all the universities and measured the hole with long tapes. And then in the end the city workmen came and made a new storm drain, and eventually the whole affair was forgotten.

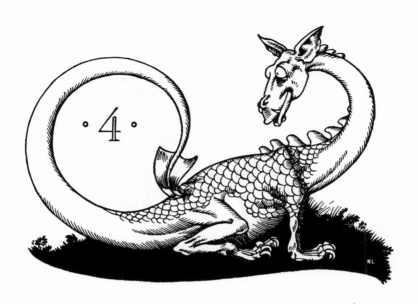

IT WAS VERY NICE for Harold (did you remember that was what Poo-Poo's other name was?) when he went to bed, because Horatio used to sleep in the garden leaning against the side of the house with his neck through Poo-Poo's bedroom window and his chin resting on the top of the chest of drawers where Poo-Poo could see him, and of course Poo-Poo was very excited and he found it hard to go to sleep, and for one reason or another Poo-Poo decided that he was going to be a very naughty boy and would do something which no good boy would dream of doing for a single moment. He got out of bed in his pajamas and looked out of the window and he thought it would be very nice to go out and find some more adventures. He knew it was very late indeed, at least nine o'clock, although he could still hear his

23

father and mother talking downstairs, because they always used to stay up very late.

He knew he didn't have a chance to get downstairs and out through the front door without their hearing him, but Horatio was grinning all over his face with a very wicked look in his eye, and so Poo-Poo pushed the window open a little bit farther and got out on the ledge. Then he sat down with one leg on each side of Horatio's neck, and then swish, he went sliding down. It was far more exciting than sliding down any banisters that he knew because Horatio's neck had big bumps all the way down it the way dragons' necks always do have. And so Poo-Poo went up-and-down — up-and-down, just like a roller-coaster —

down Horatio's neck and along his back and all the way down his tail until he fell off at the end among the nasturtiums right down by the garage. He picked himself up and brushed the dirt off his pajamas, while Horatio was very excited and went rushing round and round the garden like a whale in a goldfish bowl.

"*S-s-s-h*," said Poo-Poo to Horatio, trying to make him be quiet.

They crept round to the front of the house and went along a narrow path which grew broader and broader, and the light grew brighter and brighter until at last they were out in a big street.

On the signpost there was an arrow which showed the way to WHATEVER YOU LIKE FOR DINNER, and another arrow saying, WHATEVER YOU LIKE TO DO, and another arrow said, COME THIS WAY AND SEE WHAT HAPPENS. So Poo-Poo looked at Horatio and Horatio looked at Poo-Poo and they both looked at the arrows, and Poo-Poo said: —

"I vote we go and See What Happens."

And Horatio nodded and smiled and wagged his tail, and so off they went up the street, to where there were two springboards. And Poo-Poo went along one springboard and Horatio went along the other, and Poo-Poo (it is a long time since I asked you what his other names were) said: —

"One, two, THREE!"

And they jumped off the springboards, and they slid down through the air with the wind playing tunes around them —

25

so that Poo-Poo found himself laughing out loud and Horatio twisted his head round and laughed as well, until they fell splash! into a pool of liquid silver. As Horatio swam about in it he raised big silver waves, and as Poo-Poo swam the silver wetted his pajamas until it looked as if he were dressed in a silver suit. When they came out on the other side the bank was all glittering with diamonds which stuck to Poo-Poo's silver clothes so that as he ran about he sparkled and glittered in the light. And the great surprise was that as they ran along they found themselves at the back door again.

It was quite a job for Poo-Poo to get back into his bedroom window, because Horatio's neck was much harder to climb up than to slide down. But Poo-Poo puffed and he pulled and he pulled and he puffed as he got himself over one bump after another until at last he pulled himself up over the window and got back into bed.

He had forgotten all about his nice new pajamas until his mother asked him about them the next morning, and then he had to explain where they came from. And Poo-Poo's mother said: —

"I think they look very nice, and you can have them to wear the next time you're to stay with friends."

· 5 ·

POO–POO USED TO FIND IT very nice to go to school
nowadays, because the dragon always went with him. He was
registered as HORATIO HEAVYSIDE DRAGON (which of course was
his name. Did you remember that?) and although he was much
too big to get in the classroom, he used to lie in the playground
outside with his head in at the window and he used to listen
very attentively to everything MISS MELISANDE WINTER–
GREEN (that was the teacher's name) used to tell them about.
Sometimes the dragon would get so excited about what was
going on that he would let his tail unroll until it went right out
across the street and obstructed the traffic. And the other children used to like to have Horatio there too, because whenever

they weren't interested in what the teacher (have you forgotten her name?) was telling about, they could always turn around and look at Horatio. And during recess they used to like playing with him and climbing about on him, although of course he was really Poo-Poo's dragon.

One day a school inspector called HERBERT JEREMIAH O'SHAUGHNESSY came into the class, and he saw Horatio looking in through the window.

"What in the name of goodness is that dragon doing there?" said Mr. O'Shaughnessy, very crossly indeed.

"He's attending the class," said Miss Wintergreen.

"I don't think it's right," said the school inspector (you ought to have learnt his name by now), "that there should be a dragon in this class."

"He's on the school roll," said Miss Wintergreen. "Here's his name: HORATIO HEAVYSIDE DRAGON." (You see Miss Wintergreen never had any trouble remembering what his name was.)

"Stuff and nonsense," said Mr. O'Shaughnessy. "I never heard of such a thing before. It's just a waste of time, having dragons in a class. Go away dragon, and in the future we'll have that window shut if you please, Miss — Miss — ah . . . Miss — ah . . ." (You see, Mr. O'Shaughnessy could not remember the schoolteacher's name, and of course you do.)

So Horatio went away very sadly, and they shut the window and the class went on, and Poo-Poo felt very unhappy indeed. But recess soon came and they all went out into the playground, and there was Horatio lying down on his side in a most curious position. He had his little legs held very closely to his body and his body was quite straight, and then his tail went out into a beautiful curve behind him all the way up to his head, and he had the tip of his tail in his mouth. He lay very still and Poo-Poo was very worried about him.

First of all he ran in and he told his teacher about it. Miss Wintergreen was talking to Mr. O'Shaughnessy (of course you know who that was) and they both came hurrying out into the playground.

"All this nonsense about a dragon!" said Mr. O'Shaughnessy very crossly.

"I wish he would get up and play," said Poo-Poo unhappily.

"He's lying very still," said Miss Wintergreen, and she was obviously alarmed.

"Stuff and nonsense," said Mr. O'Shaughnessy; "I expect he's pretending."

And all the children and Miss Wintergreen, and the milkman who was going by and the postman, in fact everybody except Mr. O'Shaughnessy, all gathered round Horatio and tried to coax him to play, but he would not move at all. So Poo-Poo really began to cry.

"I'm going to fetch my father," said Poo-Poo. "He's a very clever man and perhaps he'll be able to do something for Horatio." So Poo-Poo ran all the way back home and found his father, who of course was very busy, the way it always happened whenever Poo-Poo wanted him badly.

29

"Excuse me," said Poo-Poo (I think I have told you that he was always very polite), "but do come down to the school and see what's the matter with Horatio." And Poo-Poo let a few tears fall down on the carpet and he forgot to be polite to such an extent that he wiped his nose on the back of his hand.

"Well, well, well!" said Poo-Poo's father, "I suppose I had better come along."

So they hurried down to the school where Horatio was still lying just in the same position in which Poo-Poo had left him.

"What's all this?" said Poo-Poo's father, and he walked up to Horatio, and walked around and looked at him and poked him in the ribs, and then he stood away from him and looked at him again.

"I've got it!" said Poo-Poo's father. "That's a good dragon! All right Horatio, I've seen what you're after."

And as soon as he said that, Horatio got up and all the children cheered, and Miss Wintergreen clapped her hands, and the gentleman whose last name was O'Shaughnessy snorted.

But Horatio no sooner stood up than he lay down again in another attitude. He was on his side, but this time he brought his tail in front of him, and he put out his back legs a little bit and held his tail to him just there, so that part of his tail made a sort of loop, while the tail end of it trailed away from him, and his body was still quite stiff and straight.

"That's a good dragon," said Poo-Poo's father. "Now let's have the next one."

30

So Horatio got up and lay down again, and this time he had his body and his tail quite straight and bent in an angle in the middle so as to make a sort of V upside down. And while he kept his front legs close to his body, he stretched his back legs out so as to make a bar across the Λ.

"I hope you can see what he's doing," said Poo-Poo's father to Mr. O'Shaughnessy.

"It looks a lot of nonsense to me," said Mr. O'Shaughnessy.

"Now let's have the next one, Horatio," said Mr. Brown.

And this time Horatio coiled himself nearly into an O, but just before his tail reached his mouth, he bent the tip of it back towards himself.

"Can you see what he's doing now?" said Poo-Poo's father to Mr. O'Shaughnessy.

"It almost looks as if he's making the letter G," said Mr. O'Shaughnessy.

"That's right," said Poo-Poo's father. "Come on, Horatio."

And so Horatio did not have to move very much for the next letter, and just put his tail into his mouth and made himself into a perfect O, and the next time he laid himself out straight and bent himself three ways to make himself into an N.

"My golly!" said Mr. O'Shaughnessy. "Now I see what he was doing. When we first came out here he was making the letter D. D–R–A–G–O–N. My goodness, he was spelling out his name!"

"I think that shows that he is learning a good deal at the school," said Poo-Poo's father.

"It isn't every dragon as young as that," said Miss Wintergreen proudly, "can spell out his own name."

"No, I suppose you're right," said Mr. O'Shaughnessy. And Poo-Poo had been listening to all this, although of course he should not have done so when grown-ups were talking, and so he said: —

"And can Horatio come to school with me now?"

"I suppose he can," said Mr. O'Shaughnessy.

So that was all right even though Mr. O'Shaughnessy was just as grumpy as ever (and I'm sure you can not remember what the rest of his name was).

IN THE SUMMERTIME Poo-Poo's mother used to like to have dinner in the garden. Poo-Poo used to like that, because in the garden somehow it was not quite such bad manners to get up and walk about between mouthfuls. Nobody stopped to ask Poo-Poo's father whether he liked it or not.

One day they were all having dinner in the garden when a man in a white apron came in by the garage and walked up towards them, and as soon as Horatio saw him he got up very quietly and went and hid behind a tree.

"Good afternoon, folks," said the man with the white apron.

"Good afternoon," said Mr. Brown. "I seem to remember your face, but you will pardon me if I don't remember your name."

(You see, although Mr. Brown was a very clever man he was not half as clever at remembering names as you are.)

"I am JAMES PONSONBY AUCHINLECK," said the man in the white apron, "and I am your grocer."

"Of course, Mr. — Mr. — Auchinleck," said Mr. Brown. "And what can we do for you today?"

"It's that dragon of yours," said Mr. Auchinleck very grimly.

"Oh dear," said Poo-Poo's mother. "I'm sure he's been doing something naughty."

"You're quite right, madam," said the grocer (whose name I expect you've forgotten already); "something very naughty indeed."

"What is it?" asked Poo-Poo's father.

"*He's been stealing watermelons,*" said the grocer, leaning forward so as to make quite sure Poo-Poo's father realized what a terrible thing this was.

"Has he indeed?" said Poo-Poo's father. "Here, Horatio, what have you got to say about this? . . . Horatio — bless my soul, where has that dragon gone?"

"He's hiding behind that tree," said Mr. Auchinleck (perhaps now you'll remember his name), "he knows perfectly well he's been doing what he shouldn't."

"Come out from there," said Poo-Poo's father. "I don't know what the world's coming to. First I have to have my dinner out of doors, and as if that wasn't bad enough, I have grocers and dragons and goodness knows what else coming to spoil it for me — what there is left to spoil after the wind has made it cold,

34

and the ants have eaten half of it, and the twigs have fallen into the stew. Come here, Horatio."

And Horatio came out from behind the tree with his ears hanging down and his tail trailing along the ground.

"Now let's hear what you have to say, Mr. Auchinleck," said Poo-Poo's father, "now that Horatio is present to hear the accusation."

"Well," said Mr. Auchinleck, "this morning I was dusting my watermelons and putting them out, and I thought I put out three, and when I fetched another I found there were only two. And so I went and got another one, and when I came back there were still only two. And when I fetched another one, there were still only two. So I hid behind a pile of apples and I peeped out, and in a minute or two I saw a head come round the corner on a long neck, and then — snap — there was another watermelon gone. And that was your dragon, Mr. Brown."

"Dragons can't ever resist watermelons," said Mr. Brown. "It says so in my encyclopedia. I ought to have thought of it at this time of year. What have you got to say about this, Horatio?"

Horatio never did have anything to say, but this time he clearly had less to say than ever: he just hung his head and looked down at the ground.

"There, you see?" said the grocer.

"I'm afraid I *do* see," said Mr. Brown sadly. "How many watermelons were missing?"

"I don't really know," said Mr. Auchinleck; "there you have

35

me. I couldn't say for sure. But judging by those bulges in that dragon, we ought to be able to tell quickly enough."

"So we ought," said Mr. Brown. "Come here, Horatio."

And he began to try to count the bulges down Horatio's side, but of course dragons are terribly ticklish and the moment he began to do that, Horatio threw himself down on the ground and wriggled and struggled and lashed his tail about until Mr. Brown had to give it up.

"I'm afraid we'll never be able to find out, Mr. Auchinleck," said Poo-Poo's father. "What do you propose that we do? I'm afraid I can't offer to pay you for an unknown number of watermelons."

"Something must be done," said Mr. Auchinleck.

"Well, the only thing to do is to see what Horatio says," said Mr. Brown (you remember that he was a very clever man). "Horatio, did you have one watermelon?"

And Horatio shook his head as it hung down.

"Two?" said Mr. Brown. "Three? . . . Four? . . . Five? . . ."

And each time Horatio shook his head and let it drop farther and farther down until at last Mr. Brown said: —

"Fourteen?"

And then Horatio nodded his head and looked very guilty indeed.

"Fourteen watermelons," said Mr. Auchinleck.

"Seeds and rind and all!" said Mrs. Brown, quite shocked.

36

"How much do fourteen watermelons cost?" asked Mr. Brown. "I shall have to stop it out of his pocket money."

"Well, I wasn't thinking of money," said Mr. Auchinleck. "I was thinking that perhaps the dragon would take it out in work. I'm a bit busy these days and I could do with a dragon helping me around the store."

"That's a very good idea," said Mr. Brown. "Fourteen water-melons — that means fourteen days' work. Horatio, you will start tomorrow and work for Mr. Auchinleck."

And that is just what Horatio had to do. He had to get up very early each morning and run down to the store. (Can you tell me what was the name written up on the top?) And as soon as he had tied his apron on, he was very busy indeed. You have no idea what a lot there is to be done in a grocery store. He had to crack all the apple nuts and take the apples out and stack them up in pyramids ready for sale, and he had to drop all the peas into the pods and stick the pods together, and he had to paint all the radishes red (sometimes he would miss one or two and people would find white radishes in the bunches just as you do).

He had to take all the artichoke leaves and stick them to-gether the way you expect to see artichokes, and he had to wrap the bananas up in their skins, and he had to put all the carrots into the pencil sharpener so as to put points on them. He had to dip the bunches of asparagus so as to make the ends green, and he had to roughen the tops of the cauliflower and make the green cabbages purple and the purple cabbages green, and roll up the celery stalks. The fire from his mouth was very useful for singeing the whiskers off the tomatoes so as to make them smooth. And when he had done all that, he had to sweep up all the mess he had made (which was simply terrific) — although he did it quickly enough with his tail.

When Mr. Auchinleck was tying up a parcel, poor Horatio had to be handy so that Mr. Auchinleck could cut the string on the sharp part of his back. Horatio had to deliver groceries to people's houses. And he had to help unload the truck; and then whenever he had any spare time he could always use it sawing up the packing cases for kindling with the sharp edge of his tail.

One way and another, Horatio was kept pretty busy all the time he was working for the grocer (whose name of course you remember). And Poo-Poo saw very little of him, and was quite unhappy.

But the fourteen days that Horatio had to work came to an end at last, and Mr. Auchinleck said to him: —

"We must celebrate this occasion. Let's go next door and have an ice-cream soda."

And so they went next door, and Mr. Auchinleck said to MR. QUENTIN FAZACKELY (that was the name of the man who owned the soda fountain): —

"Set 'em up, Mr. Fazackely. This is a great day and I don't mind the expense."

So Mr. Fazackely made up a great big double-dip ice-cream

soda for Horatio, and Mr. Auchinleck had a smaller one, and he and Horatio picked up their glasses — and Mr. Auchinleck said: —

"Skin off your nose and mud in your eye!"

And they drank their sodas off quick like pioneers.

It's a great sight to see a dragon drinking an ice-cream soda. When the ice cream and the cold soda get right down inside where the fire is, there is a bubbling and a hissing and a steam-

ing, and with this big ice-cream soda, the hissing was just terrific, and Horatio disappeared for a moment in the clouds of steam that surrounded him. The man behind the counter (people who knew him slightly used to call him Quentin Fazackely, but Mrs. Fazackely usually called him Q, which was much more convenient) peered at Horatio through the cloud of steam and said: —

"My golly, does that always happen when you drink a soda?"

And Horatio nodded proudly, and Mr. Auchinleck said: —

"Yes, he's a very remarkable dragon indeed."

Because during the last fourteen days Mr. Auchinleck had grown very fond of Horatio, and was proud of him as well.

"I would like to see it happen again," said Q. (That was what his wife called him, but of course you know better.) And he started in and mixed another double-dip ice-cream soda with pineapple flavoring and strawberry and rocky road ice cream, and he pushed it across the counter to Horatio. And Horatio didn't mind at all. He picked up the glass, and anybody could see that if he had been able to talk he would have said: —

"Skin off your nose and mud in your eye!"

And then up went the glass and down went the soda, and once again there was such a hissing and a bubbling and clouds of steam, as if every fire brigade in the country were trying to put out every fire there had been for the last six months.

"That's quite an advertisement for your ice-cream soda," said Mr. Auchinleck to Mr. Fazackely. And Mr. Fazackely said: —

41

"Yes, I was thinking much the same sort of thing, in fact I have a very great idea."

He turned and looked at Horatio again very earnestly.

"It looks to me," he said, "as if you liked ice-cream sodas."

And Horatio nodded his head, so Mr. Fazackely went on.

"How would you like all the ice-cream sodas you could drink?"

And Horatio nodded his head more eagerly than ever. So Mr. Fazackely went on: —

"The idea I've got is that you should sit in the window here where people in the street can see you, and whenever there's a little crowd around there, you drink a soda for them to see what happens."

And Horatio nodded again, and so it was settled. And Mr. Fazackely hurriedly made out a big poster like this: —

FAZACKELY'S SODAS

Watch and see! This is the way they cool this dragon. Just imagine what they'll do to you!!!

And he went outside and hung it over the window, and Horatio settled down behind the glass. And all this of course was very naughty of Horatio, because he was supposed to go straight home every night after working for the grocer and Poo-Poo's mother was growing quite worried about him.

But Mr. Fazackely's experiment was a very successful one indeed, because quite a big crowd collected in front of the window, and Mr. Fazackely was kept very busy making ice-cream sodas, and every time Horatio drank one there was a big "Oo — oo — oo — " from the crowd just as if a rocket had gone up, and more and more people came into the shop for ice-cream sodas.

After a time, Mrs. Brown at home said to Poo-Poo's father: — "It's nearly bedtime, and I'm worried about that dragon."

And Mr. Brown said, "Bother the dragon, can't I sit and be peaceful for the first time today? And without having to worry about a dragon?" But all the same he got out of his armchair, and Poo-Poo and he and Mrs. Brown all got into the car and drove down the hill to Mr. Auchinleck's shop to see what had happened to Horatio. As they turned the corner, Poo-Poo said:

"Just look at that crowd outside the soda fountain." And Mr. Brown said: —

"I shouldn't be surprised if that young vagabond of a dragon hasn't got something to do with that."

And of course Mr. Brown was right, the way he always was, being a very clever man, because when they parked the car and found the crowd, they could see Horatio behind the window in a cloud of steam. And as they watched, Mr. Fazackely gave Horatio another ice-cream soda, and Horatio upped with the glass and downed with the soda; but this time there was not nearly so much sizzling and steaming, and Mr. Brown said: —

"This is very serious indeed."

And he started to make his way through the crowd and into

43

the soda fountain, with Mrs. Brown behind him, and Poo-Poo behind Mrs. Brown.

Mr. Fazackely had been very disappointed at the poor results of the last ice-cream soda, and hurriedly mixed another one, so that Horatio could really show what he could do; and he was just giving it to Horatio when Mr. Brown came round behind the counter through the crowd and said, "Stop!" very loudly, and took away the glass just before Horatio could take hold of it.

Mr. Brown was very angry indeed, in fact Poo-Poo had never seen him so angry before.

"You've been taking advantage of the innocence of a poor, dumb dragon," said Mr. Brown to Mr. Fazackely.

"And as for you, Horatio, I thought you had more sense. Don't you know there's a limit to what the best-constructed dragon can stand? Supposing you had put your fire out? Where would you have been then? As it is, I don't expect there's much left of it. Let's see if you can light my cigarette for me."

Horatio looked very ashamed, and he clicked open his mouth, and he clicked it open again, and he clicked it open again, and everybody grew more and more worried until at last, when they had given up hope, there was just a little tiny gleam of flame right down inside, which you could only just see when you peeped down him.

"There, you see?" said Mr. Brown, looking angrily at Mr. Fazackely. And there was quite a murmur through the crowd.

"I've a good mind to tell the Society for the Prevention of

Cruelty to Animals about you," said Mr. Brown; "but still, I suppose it was only ignorance. But don't you ever let me find you giving dragons more than seven ice-cream sodas again, because then there'll be no excuse for you. Come along, Horatio."

And so they went out of the shop, and Horatio was all shivering and shaking with the cold of the ice cream inside, and his skin was all out in gooseflesh.

"There isn't a moment to spare," said Mr. Brown. "Run home as fast as you can, and when you get there, turn around and run back again to meet us, and then run home again, and so on until we get there. Go on, run!"

So Horatio went galloping up the street as fast as ever he could, and Mr. Brown and Poo-Poo and his mother got in the car, and Mr. Brown stepped right on the gas, and up the hill he went. And halfway up they met Horatio tearing down again, and he skidded to a stop with his claws tearing up the road, and spun around and knocked down a lamppost with his tail ("I hope nobody notices that," said Mr. Brown), and went dashing up the hill again in front of the car, and down again and up again until at last they reached home. And there was Horatio, stretched out on the lawn with his sides heaving and his tongue hanging out, and great big puffs of smoke coming out of his mouth, so that Mr. Brown was able to say: —

"That's all right. Let this be a lesson to you, young Horatio Heavyside Dragon."

(You see Mr. Brown was a very clever man, and could always remember what the dragon's name was.)

45

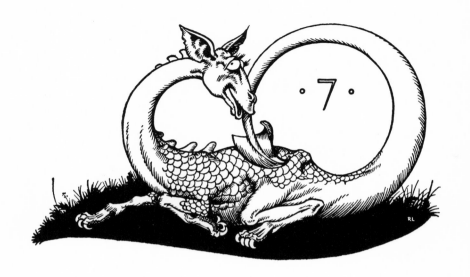

ONE DAY POO–POO and his father and mother (that's three lots of names for you to remember) were sitting out on the lawn with Horatio. And Poo-Poo was tuning in the portable radio. Of course Mr. Brown, being a very clever man, wanted to listen to the symphony concert, but Poo-Poo tuned in to the serial about Dead-Eye Dick, the Ranger of the West. Mr. Brown sat back in his chair with his eyes shut, because he said that was the best way he could think. And Poo-Poo listened to the serial, which was very exciting because Dead-Eye Dick was having a great deal of trouble with Rustlers and Indians. Poo-Poo was very careless, because he ought to have remembered about the feud there was between dragons and Indians.

Do you remember about that feud? It dates back from when Columbus discovered America. Anyway, the Indians were yelling their loudest when Horatio suddenly sat up and opened his mouth and *snap,* that radio disappeared inside him, and Mr. Brown opened his eyes just too late.

"Now isn't that a nuisance!" said Mr. Brown. But it seemed much more of a nuisance to Horatio, because the Indians went on yelling inside him, and Horatio was very puzzled and did not know what to do about it.

"I think we ought to do something about it," said Mrs. Brown.

"Oh dear," said Mr. Brown, "what with dragons and little boys there's never a minute's peace in this house."

Horatio was doubled up in a knot sniffing at the middle of himself where the Indians were yelling, until at last the yells died away gradually because Dead-Eye Dick could always fight a lot of Indians successfully. When the yells had quite finished, a voice from the middle of Horatio said very solemnly: —

"THIS IS KSFO, SAN FRANCISCO."

And some very beautiful music followed.

"It looks to me," said Mr. Brown, "as if I shall have to take that dragon round with me if I am going to listen to the symphony concert."

"I think we ought to do something about it," said Mrs. Brown again. "I shall go and telephone to DR. PACKINGHAMP-TON." (I don't expect you'll have to hear his name more than once to remember it.)

47

And so she did, and when she came out of the house again, she said to Poo-Poo, "The doctor has some time free now, and you had better walk down to see him with Horatio."

And so Poo-Poo got up, and Horatio followed him. And Poo-Poo's father said: —

"I suppose that's good-by to my symphony concert!"

Now that the Indians had left off yelling, Horatio was quite happy again, and he skipped along the street beside Poo-Poo with a man's voice singing away inside him. And as they walked down the street, they met a man walking up who was very smart indeed. He had shoes on which shone so wonderfully you could see them half a mile off, and he had a gold wrist-watch covered with diamonds, and black side-whiskers in front of his ears.

This man stopped and looked at Horatio, and then at Poo-Poo, and then back at Horatio again.

"Goodness gracious me," he said, "is this your dragon?"

"Yes," said Poo-Poo.

"Well, my name," said the man with the side-whiskers, reaching in his pockets for a visiting card, "is PERCIVAL CORO–MANDEL, a name which you have doubtless heard of." (And a name which *you* will have to remember.) "I am the proprietor of Coromandel's Great Three-Ring Circus."

"Golly," said Poo-Poo, because he had been thinking about Coromandel's Great Three-Ring Circus ever since he saw the first poster.

"This singing dragon of yours," said Mr. Coromandel, "seems to me to be rather an interesting specimen. Have you ever heard of a singing dragon before?"

"No sir, I haven't," said Poo-Poo. And as he said it, the gentleman who was singing at the broadcasting station (I think his name was GIULIO FANTOCHINI, but I am not sure)

49

went up to his top note, and Horatio positively shook with the noise that was coming out from inside of him, and so did the windows of the houses all around.

"That's fine," said the circus proprietor. "Are you and your dragon doing anything tomorrow?"

"Nothing special, sir," said Poo-Poo.

"Well," said Mr. Coromandel, "I'd like you to bring him to the circus so that other people can hear him. Can you do that?"

"Well sir — " said Poo-Poo — thoughtfully, because he was thinking about how he had to take Horatio to the doctor (whose name anybody ought to remember).

"I'll give you a lot of money," said Mr. Coromandel. "I'll give you fifty cents if you bring him."

"Well . . . " said Poo-Poo again. And he looked at Horatio and thought about the doctor, and he thought that Horatio did not look any the worse for having swallowed the radio, and that it might be all right if they waited until tomorrow before they saw the doctor; and then Poo-Poo had a very great idea, because sometimes he was clever like his father.

"Fifty cents isn't enough," said Poo-Poo. "I want to come in and see your circus free, in the best seats, and my father and my mother too."

And Mr. Coromandel groaned very deeply, but at last he said, "Very well, then, it's a bargain. Have him round at the side entrance of the circus at two o'clock tomorrow."

And with that he went on up the street, and it was just in time, because at that moment Mr. Giulio (he had a second name which you ought to remember) left off singing, and a voice deep down inside Horatio said: —

"THIS IS KSFO, SAN FRANCISCO."

But Mr. Coromandel was too far away to hear that. And Poo-Poo and Horatio trotted on down to Dr. Packinghampton (of course you remember that was the doctor's name).

Poo-Poo walked up and rang the front doorbell with the front end of Horatio beside him, while the tail end was still out in the street. And the doctor opened the door for them himself.

"Come in, come in," said the doctor, and then he looked at Horatio and added, "Well, perhaps not all of you."

So they went down the hall to the doctor's consulting room, and there Dr. Packinghampton sat down in a big chair and said: —

"Well."

And as he said that, the portable radio which was in the middle of Horatio which was out by the front door said: —

"GET A SAMPLE OF DR. PERUGIA'S POWDERS TONIGHT."

And Doctor Packinghampton said: —

"What in the name of fortune is that?"

Poo-Poo said: —

"That's what we've come to see you about, Doctor."

"Oh, yes, of course," said Dr. Packinghampton. "Mrs. Brown told me about it on the telephone.

51

"Well," said Dr. Packinghampton, "let's have a look at you. Open your mouth."

And so Horatio opened his mouth wide, and the doctor took a big spoon and held down Horatio's tongue with it.

"Say *Ah-ah-ah* . . . ," said Dr. Packinghampton to him.

And Horatio said, "Ah-ah-ah . . . ," but because he was a dragon, the moment he did that a whole sheet of flame came out from his mouth and swirled round Dr. Packinghampton's head, and if Dr. Packinghampton had not ducked immediately he would have had all his eyebrows burnt off.

"Goodness me," said Dr. Packinghampton, "that's a very serious complication."

And Poo-Poo said, "Yes, it is," which did not help Dr. Packinghampton very much. So the doctor scratched his head for a minute, and then he suddenly stood up.

"I know," he said, and went out into the kitchen and came back in half a minute with one of his wife's best extra special fireproof-glass casseroles.

"That's more like it," said Dr. Packinghampton, and he put the casserole over his face and held down Horatio's tongue once more and said, "Say *ah-ah-ah*," and the flames came out and swirled all round the casserole, but of course it did not hurt it because it was fireproof, and the doctor went on looking right down inside Horatio.

"Not so bad," said the doctor. "There is undoubtedly a portable radio down there."

And the portable radio said, "*THIS IS KSFO, SAN FRAN–CISCO.*"

And Doctor Packinghampton said, "Of course, we might have known without troubling to look down Horatio's throat, but in medicine it's best to explore every avenue. I think a light diet and not too much excitement, and we'll have a look at him again in a day or two."

"Excuse me," said Poo-Poo (he was always polite when he remembered), "I wanted to know if Horatio could perform at the circus tomorrow?"

"Circus?" said Dr. Packinghampton. "Circus? . . . Oh yes, I suppose he can, and that can't do much harm. I'll come along and see him myself! It's years since any dragon of my acquaintance performed in the circus."

And tomorrow you will hear what happened when Poo-Poo took Horatio to the circus.

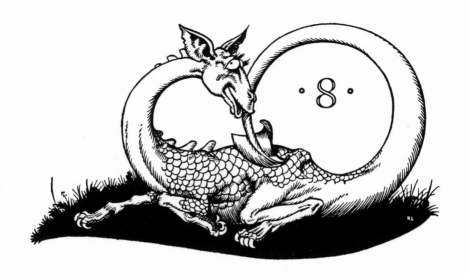

OF COURSE POO–POO was very excited when he and his father and mother and Horatio all started off for the circus, because they were going to sit in the most expensive seats there were. All along the streets there were posters up advertising the circus, with an extra poster posted across them; and on the extra poster in great big letters: —

THE ONLY SINGING DRAGON IN THE WESTERN HEMISPHERE

And when Mr. Brown saw those (what was there special about Mr. Brown to remember?) he said: —

"I hope your circus friend Mr. Coromandel isn't too disappointed, because the battery in that radio is due to run down any moment — it's been going ever since yesterday when Horatio swallowed it."

So Poo-Poo said, "Ummm," and looked out of the car window to where Horatio was going clippety-clop beside them through the traffic, which was very dense because everybody was going to the circus.

When they came to the side entrance, Mr. Coromandel was there looking quite worried, but as soon as he saw Poo-Poo and Horatio he smiled and said: —

"There you are, then!" — which was quite true.

And he said to Horatio: —

"I hope you're in good singing form today."

And Horatio said nothing at all, but inside him the radio said in just the tiniest whisper, "*This is KSFO, San Francisco.*"

And Poo-Poo was very frightened, because he knew that nobody in a big circus would hear that little whisper; Mr. Coromandel obviously didn't hear it, and he was standing right beside Horatio. But there was nothing Poo-Poo could do about it, and so he said good-by to Horatio, and he went around and joined his father and mother, and they went and sat in the most expensive seats as Mr. Coromandel had promised them.

Poo-Poo was very excited, and he looked round the big tent and he could see all his friends even though they weren't sitting in the most expensive seats the way he was.

Quite near to them there was Mr. McIntosh (do you remember who Mr. McIntosh was?), and in the next row there was Amelia Montgomery (I'm sure you know where Poo-Poo met her), and beside her there was Miss Araminta Wiggins (of course she had seen Horatio before as well, but I don't expect you can tell me where). And walking about in front in his uniform with a star, there was a policeman (Poo-Poo knew his name, and I am sure you know it too).

And across the other side there was Miss Melisande Wintergreen (Poo-Poo knew her very well, and I wonder if you can tell me why), and farther along there was Herbert Jeremiah O'Shaughnessy, still looking very cross (now that you know that he was looking cross, you can probably remember who he was).

Right up at the back there was James Ponsonby Auchinleck, sitting beside his friend, Mr. Quentin Fazackely (because they were friends you ought to know who they were), and sure enough, just as he had promised, there was the doctor (whose name you cannot have forgotten yet).

Poo-Poo jumped up and down in his seat and waved to each of these friends, while the band played very loudly with all the drums going at once and just enough trumpet to make a noise that you could hear through the drums.

And then in came Mr. Coromandel, very beautifully dressed, with a white shirt-front with three big diamonds in the middle of it, and he said: —

"Ladies and Gentlemen. It is my proud privilege to present to you today MISS FLUFFKIN SKINILIMBS, the queen of the Caucasian Desert, on her fiery untamed steed."

And the band started playing very loud again, and in came Miss Skinilimbs up on the back of her fiery untamed steed, and looking perfectly beautiful as she turned round and round and turned somersaults and jumped through hoops. And every time she jumped, Poo-Poo jumped too, and he would have turned somersaults as well, if Mr. Brown had not put out his hand and stopped him.

And after that things got too exciting for Poo-Poo ever to remember them properly. There were people on trapezes, and people climbing up ladders; and there were elephants walking around in line holding the tail of the elephant in front, and there were tigers and lots more horses, and clowns; so that Poo-Poo could hardly remember a day which he had enjoyed more especially as they were sitting right in the front in the very best seats and he could see everything.

And then the drums beat a long, long roll to show that this was a very important occasion indeed, and Mr. Coromandel came walking out with his diamonds all glittering, and he waited for the drums to stop, and then he said in a very solemn voice: —

"Ladies and Gentlemen, it is my privilege to present to you, today, the Only Singing Dragon in the Western Hemisphere.

Ladies and Gentlemen, I am a proud man at this moment, when I announce to you the entrance of Horatio Heavyside Dragon!"

And the drums rolled, and the trumpets roared, and Mr. Coromandel stood there pointing to the entrance to the ring, and in came Horatio galloping as fast as he could, and he stopped in the middle of the ring with a cloud of dust and a burst of flame, and his eyes shining like searchlights and looking very magnificent indeed, so that everybody clapped and cheered until it sounded like a storm at sea.

"I'm afraid everybody's going to be very disappointed," said Mr. Brown, "unless we can think of something very quickly to do about this."

And Poo-Poo, who had forgotten all about the radio being run down in the excitement of seeing the circus, felt very nervous and uncomfortable indeed.

"Ladies and Gentlemen — " said Mr. Coromandel — "Ladies and Gentlemen, the Singing Dragon will now sing."

And Mr. Coromandel took hold of his whip in the middle and held it out ready to beat time, and he held the other hand up without anything in it ready to beat time as well, and he looked at Horatio, and so did Mr. O'Shaughnessy and Mr. Fazackely and Dr. Packinghampton and Mr. Auchinleck and all the other people whose names of course you remember, and everybody else as well, and the circus was very still and very quiet, and they waited and waited and nobody heard a single sound. No-

58

body, that is to say, except Poo-Poo, who, because he was sitting in the best seats quite close to Horatio, could hear a little tiny weeny voice, deep down in the middle of Horatio, just whispering ever so softly: —

"This is KSFO, San Francisco . . ."

and it was such a tiny voice that Poo-Poo was the only person in the whole circus who could hear it. And after everything had been silent for a little while, somebody began to laugh, and somebody else began to laugh, and Mr. Fazackely began to laugh, and Miss Wiggins began to laugh, and even Mr. O'Shaughnessy began to smile, and the laughter grew and grew until Mr. Coromandel waved his arms and said: —

"Ladies and Gentlemen, I think this is just a simple case of stage fright. With your kind permission, we will try again."

And he raised his hands, and everybody was quiet again, and he looked at Horatio and Horatio just didn't do anything, and after a moment everybody began to laugh again, and Mr. Coromandel grew very angry, and he raised his whip and he might have done something very terrible indeed in his temper except that Horatio put out his claw and took hold of him by the shirt-front, and then Mr. Coromandel stood very still indeed, and everybody in the circus was quiet again.

And then Mr. Brown said, "Well, I suppose I shall have to do something about this. I always knew that if we once started having a dragon I'd never have another minute's peace."

And so he got up and walked into the middle of the ring

with everybody looking at him, and he held up his hand just like Mr. Coromandel, and he said: —

"Ladies and Gentlemen, on behalf of the management I must apologize for the dragon not singing. But after all, singing dragons are very ordinary things. Why, all of us have heard dragons sing at some time or other. I've thought of something else. I don't think one of us has ever heard a singing ring-master."

And everybody in the circus was still very quiet, and Mr. Brown turned to Mr. Coromandel, and he said: —

"Sing."

And Mr. Coromandel said, in a funny squeaky voice, not a bit like the voice he used to make announcements: —

"I can't."

And Horatio, who had hold of him by the shirt-front, gave him a little shake, but he still said: —

"I can't — really I can't."

So Mr. Brown said to Horatio: —

"Horatio, just show him what you can do."

And Horatio opened his mouth and let out a long tongue of flame, and began to bring it nearer and nearer to Mr. Coromandel until Mr. Coromandel said: —

"Stop, stop! I'll sing."

And then Mr. Brown turned to the audience, and he said: —

"Ladies and Gentlemen, I want to present to you the only

Singing Ringmaster in the World. Mr. Coromandel will now sing 'Pop! Goes the Weasel.' "

And then Mr. Brown turned to Mr. Coromandel and held his arms up ready to beat time, and Horatio gave Mr. Coromandel a shake, and so Mr. Coromandel started to sing "Pop! Goes the Weasel" in a funny little squeaky voice, so that everybody laughed and laughed and laughed.

And when it was all over, Mr. Brown bowed just as handsomely as Mr. Coromandel ever did, and said, "Thank you, Ladies and Gentlemen," and everybody clapped, and Horatio let go of Mr. Coromandel, and then everybody stood up and started to go out in a hurry, the way people always go out of circuses.

And Mr. Coromandel turned to Mr. Brown and said, "I am very angry indeed."

And Mr. Brown said, "I don't think you ought to be angry. Look at all the people who came."

And he told Mr. Coromandel all about Mr. Fazackely and Mr. McIntosh and Miss Wintergreen and all the other people (whose names you can remember) and Mr. Coromandel said: —

"Yes, but you had the best seats in the circus, and you didn't pay for them."

So Mr. Brown said, "There's something in that, of course."

And he put his hand in his pocket and brought out some money and he paid Mr. Coromandel for two adults and one

62

child in the best seats in the circus, and Mr. Coromandel put the money in his pocket and then he said: —

"What about Horatio? He saw the whole circus and you haven't paid anything for him."

And Mr. Brown said: "Dragons don't pay for admission to circuses. That point was decided by a Supreme Court decision in April, 1928."

And when Mr. Brown said that, Mr. Coromandel could only say, "Oh."

Because there wasn't anything more to say.

So, when they said good-by to the ringmaster (I expect you have forgotten the ringmaster's name already), they got into the car and started home with Horatio going clippety-clop behind them. And of course they were still very excited, so Poo-Poo (I hope you haven't forgotten what Poo-Poo's other names were) wriggled about in the car all the time that they were going home, and then while Poo-Poo's mother was getting supper ready, Poo-Poo and Horatio ran round and round the garden until Mr. Brown said that they made him dizzy.

And then Mrs. Brown came out to the kitchen door and called out: —

"Supper's ready!"

They all came galloping in, and between them Poo-Poo and Horatio knocked over a chair, and Mr. Brown called them a careless, clumsy, clod-hopping couple of clowns. Because Poo-Poo was so excited he was a very naughty boy, and when no one was looking he put the pepper into the salt shaker, because he knew that Horatio liked salt and did not like pepper at all.

And Mrs. Brown put Horatio's plate in front of him, and Mr. Brown remembered that Horatio liked salt; so he took the salt, and he took the salt shaker and shook it over Horatio's supper, and all the pepper came out in a stream. First Mr. Brown sneezed, and then Mrs. Brown sneezed, and then Poo-Poo sneezed; and Horatio sneezed last, although he was nearest to the pepper — because a dragon is so long that it takes a long time for the sneeze to go all the way down, and then come all the way up again. It is a wonderful thing when a dragon sneezes — because he has to straighten himself up just as you have to when you sneeze, and Horatio was coiled all the way down the garden, and when he straightened himself up, his tail went in through the kitchen door on MRS. THEODOSIA DEVER-EUX, their neighbor, and knocked over the washing machine.

And then the sneeze came all the way up again and made Horatio knock over the salt shaker, which had pepper in it, and made things worse than ever, and he sneezed and he sneezed, and Mr. Brown sneezed and sneezed, and Horatio straightened up and coiled down again with every sneeze so that the tip of his tail frightened their neighbor nearly out of her mind as it flopped about in her kitchen, until at last a really enormous sneeze came hurrying along inside Horatio, and it caught up that portable radio as it went along and it brought it out like a bullet so that it was a good thing the window was open where it went sailing through and over the trees.

And nobody ever knew afterwards what happened to it, except that Mr. Brown was never able to listen to symphony concerts again.

Mr. Brown saw the radio go, and was so surprised that he stopped sneezing and said: —

"What was that?"

And Mrs. Brown said, "I think it was the portable radio."

And they looked at Horatio, and he nodded and smiled.

And Mr. Brown said, "That's all right then!" — which was a good thing because he was so relieved at Horatio's losing the radio without having an operation that he quite forgot to ask who was the naughty boy who put the pepper where the salt ought to be.

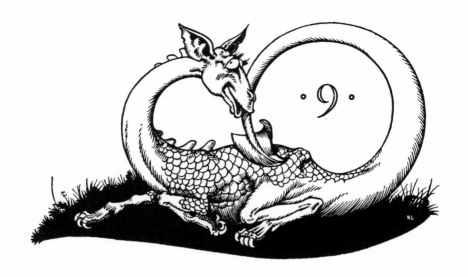

·9·

THAT NIGHT when supper was over Mrs. Brown said: —

"It's bedtime now, and you two children better have your baths."

They had a very good system for baths (I expect Mr. Brown thought of it, and you can probably explain that if you remember something important about Mr. Brown). Mrs. Brown used to put Poo-Poo in the tub and turn on the shower for Horatio. Horatio would start coming in at the side door and wind up the stairs and in through the bathroom door and under the shower and out through the bathroom window, so that a bit of himself was under the shower all the time as he moved along, and by the time Mrs. Brown had seen that Poo-Poo was properly clean and Poo-Poo had played with his boats and his celluloid swan and Mrs. Brown had taken him out and dried him, Horatio had managed to pass the whole length of himself under the shower and out through the bathroom window; and he did not need drying because as soon as he had got all of himself into the garden again he would shake himself and give Mr. Brown's flowers a good watering.

Tonight Poo-Poo was a very naughty boy again, because Mrs. Brown had hardly put him into bed and turned out the light when he got up again and went to the window and slid down Horatio's neck into the garden. It was very dark there, but Horatio switched on his searchlight eyes so that they could see very plainly, and they went along and down a wide flight of steps and up a little road until they came to some big iron railings which went along as far as they could see. And while they were looking through the railings, on the other side of them there was a scurrying and a clippety-clopping and a lot of funny noises, until suddenly another dragon appeared on the other side of the railing and came galloping up to them.

This was not quite such a big dragon as Horatio and not nearly as strong, but it was ever so pleased to see them, and it galloped up and down inside the railings, and Horatio galloped up and down the other side, and they licked each other's nose through the gaps, and they waved their tails about until the earth shook under Poo-Poo's feet with their excitement. The

67

new dragon seemed to be a very timid creature, because when Poo-Poo put his hand through the bars to stroke it, it shrank away. Poo-Poo had to talk to it for a long time, and pat Horatio with the other hand, until it would come near him so that Poo-Poo could just scratch its ears and even then it was very frightened. They made friends in the end, and Poo-Poo started to wonder how they could get round the fence to the new dragon, and he and Horatio started to walk along one side of it; and the new dragon ran along the other side of the fence beside them, galloping and zigzagging (when a dragon is zigzagging it is a very remarkable sight indeed) and waving their tails at each other, and stopping every now and then to sniff at each other's noses through the railing. And they went on and on and on, and there didn't seem to be any sign of a gate or opening in the fence at all.

But still they went on and on, because there did not seem to be anything else that they could do. Until when they seemed to have been going for a very long time, the railing came to an end, and Horatio and the new dragon were able to meet there at last, and they were able to gambol round each other and chase each other round and round in circles until Poo-Poo was quite dizzy, and he had to call to them to stop and think about the way home.

So they started off in a straight line, and pretty soon they came bump up against the railing again, and so they turned round and went in another direction, and before they could say

"Jack Robinson" (or even "Quentin Fazackely") they were up against the fence again, and after that whichever way they seemed to go they seemed to come up against that fence.

Now of course what Poo-Poo did not know (and I don't think either of the dragons knew either, but then I can't be sure) was that this fence was a very peculiar fence.

Poo-Poo and Horatio had walked along one side of it and the other dragon on the other side, and where the fence came to an end, of course, was right in the middle, so that you can see for yourself that after that whichever way they started to walk they came up against the fence. And they tried and tried and tried, until Poo-Poo was quite worried and began to feel that he would never get out of this railing at all. He even began to be afraid that the railing was moving about while he was not looking and getting into his path, but of course we know that could not be the case, because railings do not move around that way.

So in the end Poo-Poo sat down with the dragons gamboling and zigzagging all around him, and he tried to think what his father would have done if his father had been there (you know something very special about Poo-Poo's father). And when he had thought of what to do, he walked along until he came to the railing again, which did not take long, and then he made the dragons lie quite still while he looked at the tracks beside the railings. And they were much smaller tracks than the ones Horatio made, and so he knew they belonged to the other dragon, and he knew then that when he met the other dragon it was the wrong side of the fence, and so he was on the wrong side of the fence.

And so he called to the dragons and they walked along again until they reached the fence again, and there was another lot of tracks (if you think about it very carefully you will see what Poo-Poo was doing, and I think you will agree that he was nearly as clever as his father was), and these tracks were Horatio's tracks; and beside them Poo-Poo could even see his own footprints, and then he knew he had only to follow them the other way to get out of the fence, and so he walked along beside the fence, and he walked along beside it, and he walked along beside it with the dragons skipping and prancing along beside him, and then at last the fence came to an end, and Poo-Poo could heave a great big sigh because he had really been very worried about having to stay the rest of his life inside that fence.

Poo-Poo was so tired that when they reached home he hardly had the strength to climb up Horatio's neck and get back into bed, and he fell asleep the moment he was between the sheets. And he slept so soundly that he just did not remember anything about the night before when they got up in the morning, until they were having breakfast and Poo-Poo's mother looked out of the window and suddenly said: —

"My goodness, Horatio has got another dragon with him in the garden!"

And Mr. Brown put down his newspaper and said: —

"Dragons! Aren't we ever going to have any peace from dragons?" And they got up and went outside to look.

And the new dragon was very timid and shy, and it hid behind Horatio and would not come out without a great deal of coaxing. And it held down its head and looked down at the ground and wriggled in just the same way that Poo-Poo did when he met a lot of strange new people, and Mr. Brown looked at it, and he said: —

"I think this must be ERMYNTRUDE."

Because Mr. Brown, who was very clever, was especially clever at guessing dragon's names. The moment he said the name "Ermyntrude," Ermyntrude lifted up her head and smiled, and Horatio wagged his tail until all the leaves in the trees began to rustle.

And Ermyntrude got over her shyness to such an extent that she even came creeping forward and let Mrs. Brown pat her and stroke her.

But Mr. Brown said, "This is all very well, but we don't want this house to be simply overrun with dragons. We've got dragons all over the place now."

And Poo-Poo said, "Oh," very disappointedly, and Horatio left off wagging his tail.

But it was Mrs. Brown who settled that question.

She said, "Don't be silly," — quite sharply to Mr. Brown, — "I think Ermyntrude is a very nice dragon indeed." And when

71

she had said that, of course nobody else had anything to say.

They had been planning to have a picnic that day, so when Poo-Poo and his father and mother got in the car and drove out to the park, this time they had two dragons running clippety-clop behind them; and Poo-Poo was so excited, as he looked out of the window and saw them, that he wriggled about on the seat until his father had to tell him not to, because it interfered with the steering.

They went out through the big park until they came to the lake, and stopped beside the boathouse. The new dragon, of course (do you remember what her name was?), was very timid indeed. When the boathouse keeper (his name was ALO-YSIUS PENNEFATHER) spoke to her she ran away and hid behind a tree, and when the boathouse keeper's wife (I wonder if you can guess her name without being told?) came out to hang the clothes on the line, Ermyntrude crouched down, because she was frightened of all the fluttering things, even though Horatio walked up to them as brave as anything.

Poo-Poo was disappointed, because he had been hoping to have a swim with his father and mother, and now Aloysius Pennefather told them that it was too cold for anybody to go in. That was a great pity, because it was a nice sunny day and everything looked just right for swimming.

But Mrs. Brown said, "It's no good crying about the weather," and she started taking the things out of the car for the picnic.

As they were getting ready for dinner, a dog came along the edge of the lake. His name was Dots, and some people called him a Dalmatian, and some people called him an Old English Coach Dog, and some people called him a Spotted Dog, and some people called him a Plum Pudding Dog, so that you see he had quite a lot of names. But I expect that as long as you remember that he was called Dots, everything will be all right.

Dots was going for a walk by himself because none of his owners had been able to take him out that morning, and he looked up as he walked along the water's edge and he saw the two dragons playing, and because he was feeling lonely he trotted up to play with them.

The minute Ermyntrude saw him coming, of course she was very frightened, and she ran away; and Dots thought this was a very good game, and ran after her; and the faster Ermyntrude ran, the faster Dots ran, and the more frightened Ermyntrude became. And she ran faster still, and so Dots ran faster still, and Horatio ran after them because he did not want Ermyntrude to be frightened, and when he ran after Dots, Dots ran faster than ever and made Ermyntrude run faster than ever, until at last they were all three of them running along like lightning.

And Poo-Poo and his father and mother could only call after them, and they were all running so fast that they could not hear a word that was said to them. Ermyntrude was so frightened that she did not look where she was going, and she ran splash into the lake and started to swim, and Dots swam after her and Horatio swam after Dots, and they tore round and round the lake swimming as fast as they could go, raising great big waves which washed up against the beach where Poo-Poo and his father and mother were standing.

They went on round and round the lake, and they got so out of breath that they were puffing and blowing and making a tremendous noise; and of course when a dragon gets out of breath and puffs and blows, he sends out great big jets of fire from his mouth; and it was not very long before the water of the lake began to get hot and steam began to come up from it.

Aloysius Pennefather (you remember who that was) said, "We can't have this!"

And he got into a boat and rowed out among the waves and the steam; and as Dots went by, he leant out and grabbed him by the tail and stopped him, and took hold of him round the middle and pulled him out and dropped him in the middle of the boat.

When Ermyntrude found that she was not being chased any longer by Dots, she crawled up onto the bank beside Mr. and Mrs. Brown. Horatio crawled up after her, and they lay there very quietly, with their sides heaving, while the big flame that shot in and out of their mouths gradually died down as they got their breath back.

Do you remember something that I told you once about Mr. Brown? He was sitting ready to eat his picnic dinner and looking at the lake and the steam coming up from it, when all of a sudden he jumped to his feet, and he shouted out: —

"My goodness gracious me, I've got a marvelous idea!"

And he unbuttoned his collar and started pulling off his clothes, so that Poo-Poo and his mother thought there was something very serious the matter with him. But of course there was not, because Mr. Brown was a very clever man, and had just had a very good idea.

"Where is my bathing suit?" said Mr. Brown. "That water's nice and warm."

Don't you think that was a very good idea?

In a moment Poo-Poo and his mother and father had their bathing suits on, and they rushed down to have a swim. It is ever so nice to swim in a great big lake quite full of really warm water. They swam about very happily while Mr. Aloysius Pennefather (can you remember what his job was?) got on the telephone and started to telephone to everybody he knew, about how warm the lake was. And they all got into their automobiles; and the people who did not have motor cars got into buses and trains or called up their friends who did have automobiles; and they all came pouring into the park. And soon they all were swimming and enjoying themselves, as happy as could be.

After Poo-Poo and his father and mother had had their swim and were sitting having a picnic lunch, and Poo-Poo was feeling very clean indeed, a whole lot of people dressed in their best clothes came up to them. In the front of the procession was MR. SEBASTIAN FITZALLAN, who was the Mayor of the City. And the Mayor (he is a very important man, so whatever you do you must not forget his name) had very beautiful manners, and he took off his hat and bowed, and he said: —

"I beg your pardon for interrupting you at your dinner, but I have come in the name of the City, to thank Mr. Harold Heavyside Brown" (Poo-Poo wondered for a moment who that was) "for the kindness he has shown to this community in allowing his dragons to warm up the lake so that we could all have a swim. In the presence of all these witnesses, I HEREBY CON–FER UPON MR. HAROLD HEAVYSIDE BROWN THE FREEDOM OF THE CITY."

And everybody cheered.

And Mrs. Brown poked Poo-Poo under the table to remind him to stand up and say, "Thank you very much."

To which of course the Mayor (because he was so important I hope you have not forgotten what his name was) replied, "You're very welcome."

So that what with one thing and another, it was a very re-markable day.

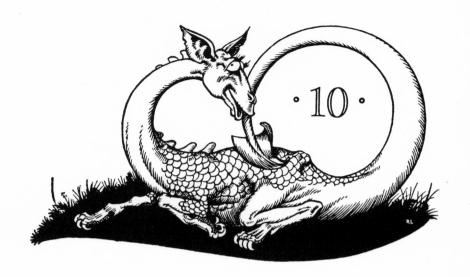

· 10 ·

WHEN THE SUN was beginning to set and the picnic day
was over, Mr. Brown said, "We'll have to think about bedtime
and go home," which is the thing that has to be said one way or
another at the end of every day.

So Poo-Poo and his father and mother got into the car and
drove towards the city with the two dragons (it seems a long
time since I asked you what the dragons' names were) running
along clippety-clop behind them.

Poo-Poo said, "Let's go home through the tunnel."

And Mr. Brown said, "I've never seen such a boy in all my
life! He's not satisfied with being given the Freedom of the

City, but on the very same day he wants to go through a tunnel. . . . Well, I suppose we will."

(The tunnel was one way of going back into the city, under a big hill, and it was really two tunnels, one for traffic out of the town and one for traffic into the town. Poo-Poo used to like to go through it because he used to try to see if he could hold his breath all the time they were going through it from one end to the other. And sometimes he did and sometimes he didn't.)

So they got onto the main road, which was full of the evening traffic streaming along in both directions, and they went along it towards the tunnel, with the dragons going clippety-clop behind them. And along behind the dragons came an enormous truck — which was driven by a man called GEORGE FABRI-CIUS MARTINELLI, who was in a terrible hurry; and he drove his big truck close up behind Ermyntrude and blew his horn very loud and frightened poor Ermyntrude nearly out of her wits. So she gave one jump and landed on the wrong side of the road, and just ran and ran and ran — with Horatio after her trying to comfort her — and the traffic that was coming the other way went skidding off the road this way and that, as they saw the two dragons galloping along the wrong side of the road; and Poo-Poo's father said: —

"I suppose I ought to have thought of that. I don't think I have been as clever as usual."

They watched the dragons go galloping up the road, and

they saw them disappear up the tunnel, going the wrong way; and Mr. Brown said: —

"My golly, we'll have to do something about this!"

So he stepped on the gas and drove the car very fast indeed — so fast that he left the big truck which had caused all the trouble a long way behind him (you know the name of the truck driver); and they whizzed through the tunnel so fast that Poo-Poo could easily have held his breath from one end to the other if he had remembered about it; but of course this time he had forgotten it, because he was worried about the two dragons.

When they came out on the other side, it was a terrific sight. All the traffic into the other tunnel was held up for miles and miles, and all the drivers were blowing their horns as loud as they could.

Mr. Brown said: —

"It'll take from now till next Friday to straighten all this up — possibly even Saturday."

He stopped the car beside the road, and they all got out and walked across to the other tunnel. And the horns were making such a noise that they could not even hear themselves think. And while all the horns were blowing there was also the noise of a siren — and along came a motorcycle, and it stopped in the middle of the traffic jam and a policeman (whose name I am sure you remember) got off the motorcycle and said: —

"WHAT'S ALL THIS?"

And none of the drivers could tell him, so they simply blew

80

their horns louder than ever; so that Policeman Macgillicuddy (that was the name, wasn't it?) could not hear himself think either.

Mr. Brown went up to him and shouted into his ear through the roar of the horns: —

"I think it's a dragon got stopped in the tunnel."

"A dragon?" said Policeman Macgillicuddy. "It feels more like an earthquake to me."

And sure enough, the ground under their feet was trembling just as if there were an earthquake.

"I can't explain the earthquake," shouted Mr. Brown, "but I can assure you that a couple of my son's dragons went up the other end of the tunnel and haven't come out of this end."

"Oh, *did* they?" said the policeman (what was his name again?). "We'll have to see about that."

But the policeman was a very big man, and the tunnel was just jammed tight with traffic, and there wasn't a chance of his getting through so that he could see about it. And Mr. Brown was a very big man as well. So in the end they said to Poo-Poo: —

"Come along, Poo-Poo, go up the tunnel and see what's happened to Ermyntrude."

So Poo-Poo got down on his stomach, and he wriggled along underneath trucks and underneath automobiles and around wheels until he came to the middle of the tunnel. And there was a bus standing quite still, and beyond the bus there was

Ermyntrude, facing towards the bus, and shaking so much with fright that it explained why Policeman Macgillicuddy thought there was an earthquake going, and behind Ermyntrude there was Horatio trying to comfort her, but because Horatio could only comfort her tail end, it was not much good, because it never is much good trying to comfort the tail end of a dragon.

Poo-Poo could see at once that it would be no good trying to get Ermyntrude to back up down the tunnel while she was as frightened as that. And so he crawled back round the wheels and under the exhaust pipes all the way to where his father and Policeman Macgillicuddy were having an argument, and he told them how matters stood. So Policeman Macgillicuddy had to back up all the traffic. And, because there was a solid block five miles long, he had to dash up and down a long time on his motorcycle to make the ones farthest back back up first, and then the next ones and then the next ones; and all the horns were roaring away until at last the bus came backing out of the tunnel full of very cross passengers. And then at last Poo-Poo could go up the tunnel again and lead Ermyntrude out with Horatio behind her, and Ermyntrude looked very sorry for herself, and all the traffic started pouring out the tunnel once more, and as each car went past them it blew its horn to show what it thought of them, so that Ermyntrude nearly jumped out of her skin each time.

And Policeman Macgillicuddy took out his notebook and

his pencil, and licked it, the way his mother always told him not to do, and said: —

"There's going to be trouble for you over this business."

And Mr. Brown said, "Oh, no there won't."

"And why not?" asked the policeman (you have just heard his name).

"My son, Harold," said Mr. Brown (perhaps you can guess who Mr. Brown's son Harold was), "has just been given the Freedom of the City, and anyone who has the Freedom of the City can take his dragons up tunnels the wrong way. It says so in the Constitution."

"Does it now?" asked Policeman Macgillicuddy.

"Yes, it does," said Mr. Brown. "If you will take my advice, you won't attempt anything contrary to the Bill of Rights. That would be a very serious thing for a policeman to do. I am surprised that you are so ignorant of the Constitution as to suggest such a thing."

"I'm surprised too," said Policeman Macgillicuddy.

"Well, that's all right then," said Mr. Brown, "good evening."

He got back into the car, and so did Mrs. Brown and so did Poo-Poo; and they drove off home with the dragons going clippety-clop behind. And because of all the delay it was long past bedtime when they got home.

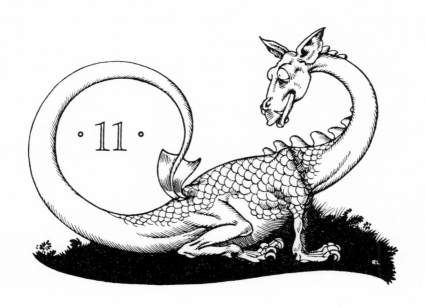

ONE MORNING Mrs. Theodosia Devereux, who lived across the road, telephoned to Poo-Poo's mother and said: —

"Something terrible has happened, I have lost Marmaduke!" MARMADUKE PRENDERGAST DEVEREUX was the name of Mrs. Devereux's baby son, who was only six months old, and who was doing his best to grow as long as his name.

"Dear oh dear oh dear!" said Mrs. Brown on the telephone. "How *ever* did this happen?"

"I don't know," said Theodosia (that is what Mrs. Brown called her because she knew her very well, but we usually have

85

to say something else). "I left him in his baby carriage just outside the house, and when I came out he was gone."

"What about the baby carriage?" asked Mrs. Brown.

"That was gone too," said Mrs. Devereux.

"Well," said Mrs. Brown, "if he took his baby carriage with him, he ought to be all right."

"But supposing he's been kidnaped!" said Mrs. Devereux.

"I hadn't thought of that," said Mrs. Brown. "Have you telephoned the police?"

"I'll do that directly," said Mrs. Devereux.

"And I'll go and talk to my husband while you telephone," said Mrs. Brown.

So Mrs. Brown went along to her husband, and Mr. Brown sighed and said: —

"What is the trouble now? I suppose it's either dragons or little boys."

"No, it isn't either," said Mrs. Brown. "This time it's a baby. Marmaduke is missing."

And Mrs. Brown told Mr. Brown everything that Mrs. Devereux had just told her, and ended up by saying how she had advised Mrs. Devereux to call the police.

"That's a pity," said Mr. Brown, getting up out of his chair very hurriedly and putting down his newspaper. "It might have been just as well to have kept the police out of this, because I have my suspicions. Have you seen Ermyntrude lately?"

"Now you come to mention it," said Mrs. Brown, "I haven't. Poo-Poo and Horatio are playing in the garden, but Ermyntrude isn't there."

"Just what I expected," said Mr. Brown, very cross indeed. "Didn't you know that in female dragons the maternal instinct is very highly developed? That means they just love children. Run and tell Mrs. Devereux quickly, and tell her not to telephone the police. I'll go and get the car out."

But when Mrs. Brown got through to Mrs. Devereux, she found that it was already too late, because Mrs. Devereux had already telephoned the police, and you know that once the police start on a case, especially to do with kidnaping, they never relax their hold.

So Mr. Brown and Mrs. Brown and Poo-Poo all jumped into the car, and the other dragon ran along behind them, and they tore round the streets looking for Ermyntrude, and the baby (who was not quite as long as his name, which I expect you remember), and after a little while they went round a corner and there was Ermyntrude, walking very proudly along the street pushing the baby carriage in front of her, holding her head up very high in the hope that everybody would think that Marmaduke Prendergast Devereux was her baby.

Marmaduke was sitting up in his carriage very pleased at having a dragon to take him out for a walk, and he was waving his rattle, and every now and then he would drop it over the

side for Ermyntrude to pick up because it made him very proud
to have a dragon picking up his rattle. And Ermyntrude was
very glad to pick it up, because that might make people think
that he was her baby. And so they were both of them very

88

pleased with each other, and when the automobile stopped beside them, and Mr. Brown jumped out of the car looking very angry, both Ermyntrude and the baby were very disappointed.

"You're a naughty girl," said Mrs. Brown to Ermyntrude.

"You're easily the naughtiest dragon I've ever had anything to do with," said Mr. Brown. And Ermyntrude hung her head and dropped her ears and wrinkled up her nose because she was very disappointed and felt like crying. And Marmaduke took one look at Mr. Brown and threw his rattle away and started to yell as loudly as he could, which was very loudly indeed, and he would not stop even though Mrs. Brown patted him on the back and said, "There, there," and joggled the baby carriage up and down.

And the big tears came pouring out of Ermyntrude's eyes, and Horatio came beside her and tried to be sympathetic, and looked very sad, until at last Mr. Brown tore his hair and said: —

"I've never seen a minute's happiness since I began to be plagued with all these dragons and little boys!"

And Mrs. Brown joggled the crying baby with one hand and stroked Ermyntrude with the other, and said: —

"It's all your fault, because you looked so cross."

Because of course she took sides with Ermyntrude, because they both had the maternal instinct. And Poo-Poo took sides with Horatio, the way little boys and dragons always do help each other, so there Mr. Brown was, left all alone in the argument.

And just at that moment, around the corner of the street came a motorcycle, and that made Mr. Brown crosser than ever, and he said: —

"There, you see? If you hadn't wasted all this time we could have got away before the police came."

So, when the motorcycle stopped and the policeman (his first name was Patrick, and I'll leave it to you to say what his second name was) got off the motorcycle and came towards them, Mr. Brown was in no mood to be trifled with. The policeman took out his pencil and notebook and Mr. Brown said, quick as lightning: —

"If you lick that pencil just once, I'll report you to the Higher Authorities."

And that was very disturbing to the policeman and he stood with his pencil halfway up to his lips, so taken by surprise that he could not even say, "WHAT'S ALL THIS?" as he had meant to say.

And if anyone had thought that Marmaduke was yelling loudly because of Mr. Brown, he should just have heard him when he saw Policeman Macgillicuddy. There never was such a din as he raised.

So Mrs. Brown turned on Policeman Macgillicuddy and said, "Can't you see you're frightening the child?"

And Poo-Poo said, "Why are all your buttons undone?"

Policeman Macgillicuddy had been sitting in his shirt-sleeves when the telephone call came about the kidnaping, and he had jumped on his motorcycle without waiting to do his buttons up; and of course it is a terrible thing for a policeman to appear in public with his buttons undone.

Now Ermyntrude, who did not understand at all what was going on except that the policeman was frightening the baby, left off crying and pushed in between the policeman and the baby carriage, looking very fierce because of her maternal instinct; and Horatio pushed up alongside her to protect her, looking fiercer still; so that Policeman Macgillicuddy felt very lonely and looked up and down the street for help; and, to help himself think, he was just going to lick his pencil when Mr. Brown said: —

"DIDN'T I TELL YOU NOT TO DO THAT?"

So that he was just not able to think at all, especially with Marmaduke Prendergast Devereux making so much noise that not even a very clever man could think very much.

But there was a very decided advantage about Marmaduke's crying, because his mother heard the noise as she was running distractedly about the streets, and she came flying around the corner.

She caught up Marmaduke from the baby carriage and patted his back and said, "There, there," just like Mrs. Brown; and then she said, "Don't cry, Marmaduke, Mummy's here."

And Mrs. Brown said, "This big brute of a policeman has frightened the child!" so that Mrs. Devereux turned on the policeman as well and said, "It's a perfect disgrace!" and then she said, "Never mind, Marmaduke, did the nasty old policeman frighten you?"

Then she turned back to the policeman and said, "I don't know what the world is coming to when policemen go about the streets frightening little children." And she said a great many more things before the policeman could think of anything to say at all (I very much doubt if he could remember his own name, but of course you can).

But at last he was able to say, "I beg your pardon, madam, but didn't you telephone for me?"

And Mrs. Devereux said, "Of course I telephoned, but I expected intelligent assistance, and not a great big brute like you."

And by that time Marmaduke's yells had changed to hiccups and she put him back in his carriage and started to walk away very indignantly.

And Mr. and Mrs. Brown and Poo-Poo got into the car and drove off, and the dragons went along the road very sedately. And it was not until they were all out of sight around the corner that the policeman began to recover his senses and, even then, what Mr. Brown had said about licking his pencil so disturbed him that he could find no pleasure in doing it now, and so he could not think of anything to do, and so he didn't do anything, and Ermyntrude came alongside Mrs. Devereux as she pushed the baby carriage, and she looked so pleading that Mrs. Devereux let her push it.

And Ermyntrude walked along very proudly, hoping that people would think that Marmaduke Prendergast Devereux was really her baby.

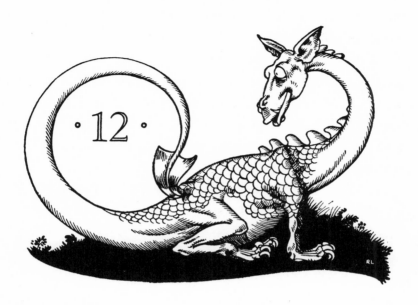

SOMETIMES POO–POO was a very lucky boy, and this time he was lucky because of something about his father (can you remember Poo-Poo's father's name, and anything special about him?). Of course, besides being lucky, Poo-Poo also had to be good, in order to give his luck a chance. He had been very good for a long time, and so had Horatio, and so had Ermyntrude, and because they had been so good, Poo-Poo's father said they could have an extra-special treat. Then Poo-Poo started to be lucky, because his father was such a clever man that when he started to think about an extra-special treat, it really was an extra-special one.

Mr. Brown told them all, one morning, that he had taken a

steamer for the day, and they would go for a cruise in the bay, just wherever they liked. Of course that made Poo-Poo and Ermyntrude and Horatio very much excited, although they were not nearly so excited as Mr. Brown was. Anybody seeing them would have thought it was Mr. Brown's treat, and not Poo-Poo's and Horatio's and Ermyntrude's. And Mrs. Brown bustled about and packed up a tremendous lunch for all of them with special baskets of this and that and the other thing for the dragons, and a reserve basket of something else in case they ran short. And at Mr. Brown's suggestion she packed a very special lunch indeed for CAPTAIN WELLINGTON SIMPKINS, who was the Captain of the ship, and for MR. AGAMEMNON FEATHERSTONE, who was the Engineer. (But Captain Simpkins called him "Aggie," and he called Captain Simpkins "Welly," which made it much more convenient for everybody.)

So they went down to the pier, and there was the ship waiting for them with the Captain and the Engineer standing on the deck looking out for them. And Poo-Poo and Ermyntrude and Horatio came galloping on board, and Mr. Brown galloped after them just as if it was his own treat instead of Poo-Poo's and the dragons', and Mrs. Brown came after him much more sedately, although she was very excited too.

And Mr. Brown said, "Cast off and hoist the mainsail," as if he were Columbus and Lord Nelson rolled into one.

So they let go of the ropes which held the ship to the pier, which is what is meant by the expression, "Cast off." It shows what a clever man Mr. Brown was. But they did not have any mainsail to hoist, which shows he was not so clever after all.

But Mr. Featherstone (do you remember what his job was?) went and started up the engine, which was just as good or even better, and off they went across the bay.

And Mr. Brown walked up and down the deck singing "A Life on the Ocean Wave" louder than Columbus ever did, and Poo-Poo and the dragons ran round and round the ship without stopping. And Mrs. Brown found a quiet chair and sat down in it and really enjoyed herself. And it was a lovely day, and the sun shone and nothing could have been better.

And the Captain touched his cap to Mr. Brown and said: —
"Where to, sir?"

And Mr. Brown said, "Lay me a course for Underagumbo Island," very nautically indeed.

And the Captain looked doubtful and said: —
"Underagumbo is a bit far, sir."

And Mr. Brown said very loftily: —
"That's why I chose it."

So the Captain whistled down the speaking tube to the engine room, and when the Engineer (of course you know what his name was) answered, the Captain said: —
"The gentleman wants to go to Underagumbo, Aggie."

And the Engineer answered: —
"Underagumbo's a bit far, Welly."

And the Captain said, "That's just what *I* was saying to the gentleman," and he looked at Mr. Brown.

And Mr. Brown was very lofty indeed, and he said, "When I say Underagumbo, I mean Underagumbo."

(It's very hard to imagine anyone saying Underagumbo if he didn't mean it, because it's not the sort of word anyone would say by accident or by mistake.)

Captain Simpkins shrugged his shoulders and said, "Very well then, sir," and he went to the wheel and laid a course for Underagumbo.

And so they went right out into the middle of the bay, and the water became rougher and rougher, and the ship began to wiggle-waggle, and quite soon Mr. Brown left off singing and became strangely quiet, and Horatio and Ermyntrude left off running about and became very quiet too, and just wanted to lie still on the deck. And Ermyntrude put her chin on Mrs. Brown's lap, and Mrs. Brown looked down at her and said: —

"My goodness, Ermyntrude, you're looking quite green."

And Ermyntrude did not say anything at all. And then Mrs. Brown looked round at Horatio, and she said: —

"My goodness, Horatio, you're looking green too."

And Horatio didn't say anything at all, but just lay very still.

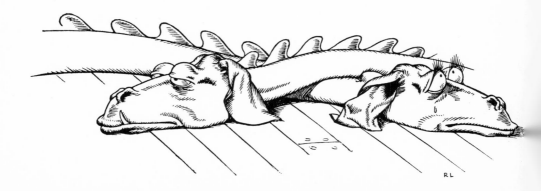

And then Mrs. Brown caught sight of Mr. Brown, and she said, "My goodness, you're looking green too, dear!"

And Mr. Brown said, "Yes, as a matter of fact, I don't feel very well."

And then Mrs. Brown looked at Poo-Poo, and Poo-Poo was just as green as Horatio and Ermyntrude.

And Poo-Poo said, "I think I'm going to be seasick," and he was.

And Mrs. Brown said cheerfully, "Well, well, well, as long as that is all that's the matter with you, I shan't worry. In fact I'm going to have some lunch."

And she got out the baskets and she ate a lovely lunch, and Captain Simpkins and Mr. Featherstone came and sat beside her and ate their lunch too, and enjoyed every mouthful of it, while Mr. Brown and Poo-Poo and Horatio and Ermyntrude were very sorrowful indeed.

Mrs. Brown tried to tempt the dragons to eat their lunch, but it was no use at all. They wouldn't have any of this or that or the other thing, and when Mrs. Brown went to the special basket and got out something else and offered it to Horatio, he turned his head away, and Ermyntrude shut her eyes and just looked more sorrowful than ever.

And Poo-Poo said: —

"When we get to Underagumbo I shan't *ever* want to come back again."

But when they got to the island (I don't think I've ever asked you what the island was called), they began to cheer up. And the Captain dropped the anchor and put out the gangplank, and they all went tumbling on shore. And they galloped over the rocks, and they climbed up to the top and looked back across the bay to where they could see their house on the top of the hill, and soon they were all so cheerful that Mrs. Brown said: —

"I think we'd better have another lunch."

So they brought the baskets ashore, and sat in a row, and the dragons ate this and that and the other thing, and the Captain and the Engineer called each other Welly and Aggie, and Poo-Poo made up for being seasick.

And Mrs. Brown said to her husband, "You're looking much better, dear."

And Mr. Brown said, very indignantly, "You talk as if I'd been ill."

And that just goes to show that Mr. Brown was just like anyone else, even though he was a very clever man.

And after lunch the dragons did some fishing, the way dragons do. It was a little uncomfortable for them, but because they were so fond of fishing, they did not mind. They had to double themselves up beside the water so that they could look into it, at the same time that their tails hung over it, and then the minute a fish came by they would whip out their tails like lightning into the water and spike the fish with the arrowhead on the tip, and haul him out, and they caught a lot more fish than Poo-

Poo did, or the Captain did, or the Engineer did, or even than Mr. Brown did. And when they had caught all the fish they wanted, they had a swim.

Then when the sun was getting low, Mr. Brown woke up with a jerk and said: —

"All aboard. Up anchor. All hands to the main-royal."

So they started for home, which was what Mr. Brown meant. And it was lucky that the wind had fallen, or something had happened to the tide, or something like that, because now the bay was quite smooth, and the ship did not wiggle-waggle at all, and everybody felt quite well. And Mr. Brown sang "A Life on the Ocean Wave" more loudly than ever.

But when they were right out in the middle of the bay, Aggie (I expect you remember who he was) called up the speaking tube and said, "We're getting a bit short of fuel, Welly," and the Captain (you had better remember what his name was because you will need it in a moment) said: —

"What do you mean by that, Aggie?"

And the Engineer said, "What I mean is we are going to stop right dead here in the middle of the bay in two minutes."

And the Engineer was quite right, because in two minutes the engine stopped, and the ship lay quite still in the middle of the bay. And the Engineer came up from down below, and the Captain came down from the bridge, so that they met on the deck, and were very angry with each other.

"This makes me very cross indeed, Mr. Featherstone," said the Captain. He called him Mr. Featherstone because he was angry.

"I gave you warning before we started out, Captain Simpkins," said the Engineer.

He called him Captain Simpkins because he was angry too, (and so now you know why you had to be ready with the Captain's name).

"It's a perfect disgrace, Mr. Featherstone," said the Captain.

"I agree with you, Captain," said the Engineer spitefully.

Then the Captain said, "I think it was all the gentleman's fault."

"So do I," said the Engineer.

And they turned round and looked at Mr. Brown who left off singing "A Life on the Ocean Wave" and said: —

"What's the matter, why don't we clew up the spanker and go home?"

And the Engineer said, "The engine won't do any more clewing, Mr. Brown."

And the Captain said, "We've run out of fuel, Mr. Brown."

And they looked so cross that Mr. Brown knew he would have to do something about it.

"That's nothing," he said. "There's never any trouble about getting home from anywhere if only you remember to bring a couple of dragons along. And I seem to remember seeing a couple of dragons on board somewhere."

And, of course, no sooner had he said that, than Horatio put his nose into one of his hands, and Ermyntrude put her nose into the other. So Mr. Brown looked down and said: —

"Of course, I knew there were a couple of dragons somewhere about. Come along with me, and let's get this old ship back to the pier."

So he took them into the middle of the ship, and he made them lie down across the deck with their noses together, and Ermyntrude's tail hanging down into the water on one side, and Horatio's tail hanging down into the water on the other side. And Mr. Brown fetched himself a chair, and he sat down beside the dragons' noses. And he began to tell them a story. It was the most wonderful story Horatio and Ermyntrude had ever heard, because it was all about the things that sensible dragons like best.

First of all, it was about watermelons, and then it was about ice-cream sodas, and then it grew more and more exciting, and Mr. Brown told them about a very lucky dragon who bit into a watermelon and found it full of ice-cream soda, and Horatio and Ermyntrude grew more and more excited as the story went on, and they wagged their tails which hung down in the water, and they wagged them and wagged them, faster and faster as the story grew more exciting, so that they were just like paddle-wheels on each side of the ship, and the ship was tearing

along as fast as ever it could, and the Captain (do you remember what the Engineer called him when he was not angry?) had to run up to the wheel fast, and the Engineer (the Captain had two names for him) was ever so happy because he had never been out in that ship before without having to be in the engine room, and now he could sit on the deck and let the wind blow past him and enjoy himself and listen to the story Mr. Brown was telling the dragons.

So the old ship went tearing across the bay so fast that there were great white waves around her bows, and people on shore looking out thought what a wonderful man the Engineer must be to make her go along as fast as that; and of course they were wrong, because it was all Mr. Brown's doing. (And you can remember something very special about Mr. Brown which explains it.)

And after a little while the Captain shouted down from the bridge: —

"Mr. Brown, we're not going quite straight, and I want to turn the ship a bit; can you go slow with the starboard paddle?"

And Mr. Brown said, "Easily."

And so in his story he started talking about babies, and that made Ermyntrude's tail go very fast indeed, because of her maternal instinct, and it made Horatio's tail go slowly because he was not very interested in babies, and because of that the ship swung round.

And very soon the Captain called out: —

"That's enough, sir," and then, "That's too much, sir," because the ship was going too far round.

And so Mr. Brown said, "All right."

And so he changed the story round until he was talking about Dalmatian dogs. (Can you remember the name of the Dalmatian dog?) So Ermyntrude left off wagging her tail for a moment, because she did not like Dalmatian dogs at all, and pretty soon the Captain called out: —

"That's all right, sir."

And so Mr. Brown dropped the Dalmatian dog out of his story just the same way as it dropped out of one of the stories in this book. (In fact it might have been that story Mr. Brown was telling them, for all I know.) And he went on talking about all the things a dragon likes, and the tails went on wagging, and the ship went on tearing across the bay, until the pier was quite near.

And then Captain Simpkins shouted out, "Way enough," which meant, "That'll do," but sailors never say things the way other people say them.

And so Mr. Brown hurriedly said, "And that's the end of the story."

And the dragons' tails ceased to wag, because they were very sorry the story had come to an end, and the ship went on slowly up to the pier, and the Engineer (his friends called him by a name much shorter than his real name) threw a rope to the people who were looking on, and they bumped gently against the pier and the voyage was over. And the dragons were very, very tired.

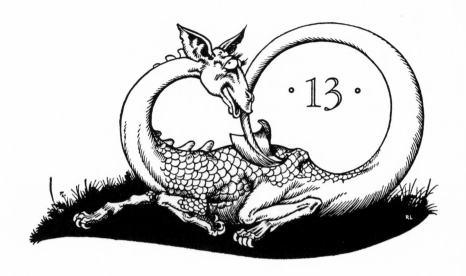

SO WHEN THEY WERE ALL on the pier again, and had said good-by to the Captain and the Engineer (the Engineer was very sorry to see them go, because he had enjoyed Mr. Brown's story just as much as Ermyntrude and Horatio and Poo-Poo had), Mrs. Brown said: —

"Now that we are in town, I had better do some shopping before we go home, because it will save a journey."

And Mr. Brown said, "Oh!"

Because one of the things that Mr. Brown disliked more than anything else was shopping, which meant waiting about while Mrs. Brown did it. And Mrs. Brown said to him: —

"That's all right, my dear, you won't have to wait about for me, because it's time you got your hair cut."

And Mr. Brown said, "Oh!" again, louder than ever, because he disliked getting his hair cut even more than he disliked waiting around while Mrs. Brown did the shopping.

Although Mr. Brown was very tired and very cross, and just hated the thought of having his hair cut, he looked at the two dragons and he said to them: —

"You have been very good dragons. Even although I am a very clever man" (did you remember that about Mr. Brown?) "it would have puzzled me how to get the ship home if I hadn't had you to help me. So while I am getting my hair cut, and Mrs. Brown is shopping, you spend this on whatever you like."

And he put his hand in his pocket, and he gave Horatio some money, and he gave Ermyntrude some money, and then he looked at Poo-Poo (it's a long time since I asked you what Poo-Poo's other name was) and he went on: —

"And you've been a very good boy, too, Poo-Poo, and so here's an extra week's pocket money for you too."

And the dragons and Poo-Poo were very pleased indeed, and the dragons forgot that they were tired, and Mr. Brown felt very noble, and he said to himself: —

"Everybody is going to enjoy themselves: Mrs. Brown is going to buy steak, and she'd rather buy steak than do anything else in the world. And Horatio and Poo-Poo and Ermyntrude are going to buy things for themselves, while I am going to get my hair cut, and there is nothing more in the whole world that I hate doing. So everybody is happy except me, and I shan't complain."

And he felt very noble and went away to get his hair cut, while Poo-Poo and the dragons went skipping along towards the shops.

Poo-Poo and Horatio wanted to buy just the same kind of things, and they spent their money very quickly on toy boats and ice-cream cones, and Poo-Poo tried to help Ermyntrude spend her money, but that was very difficult. She did not want toy boats or ice-cream cones, and when Poo-Poo took her to the other counter and offered her dolls and toy furniture, she would not buy them. In fact, she was being very difficult, and Poo-Poo thought there was something the matter with her.

He offered her this and he offered her that, and each time she would not buy them. So at last they came out of the shop, and Poo-Poo said to her: —

"Well, Ermyntrude, what *do* you want?"

And Ermyntrude promptly trotted up the street with Poo-Poo and Horatio running after her, wondering what she had in her mind, and then suddenly Ermyntrude stopped outside the beauty parlor of Madame Yvonne de Paradis, and Poo-Poo for the life of him could not guess what Ermyntrude wanted. But there she stood looking anxiously at the door, and Poo-Poo said: —

"You don't want to go in there, do you, Ermyntrude?"

And Ermyntrude nodded her head very frantically indeed.

So Poo-Poo said, "All right, then," very puzzled, and he pushed open the door, and he and Ermyntrude started going in side by side, with Horatio trying to follow them, and just as puzzled as Poo-Poo was. And when they got inside, it was a very puzzling place too, because wherever they looked they saw women with sheets round them sitting with things like saucepans on their heads, and each time they pushed open a door, and saw one of these women, the woman squawked, and they went out again hurriedly and tried another door.

And then Madame Yvonne de Paradis came up to them and said: —

"Well, what do you want? This isn't any place for little boys, or for dragons."

And she looked back all along Ermyntrude's length, and at the far end she could see Horatio very puzzled, and she went on and said: —

"My goodness, how many of you are there?"

And Poo-Poo said, "It doesn't matter about Horatio, it was Ermyntrude who wanted to come in here."

And Yvonne (have you learnt the rest of her name yet?) said, "Oh, this is Ermyntrude, is it? Of course that's a very different matter. I expect she wants a beauty treatment."

And Ermyntrude nodded and smiled.

"But have you got any money?" said Madame de Paradis, very firmly, because she was a good business woman.

And Ermyntrude nodded and smiled again, and held out her money. And Madame de Paradis took it and counted it and said: —

"That makes it quite all right. Just step this way, please."

So she opened the door for Ermyntrude to go in, and then she turned back to Poo-Poo.

"This is certainly no place for little boys," she said, "and it's no place for Horatio, either. A beauty parlor is very strictly For Ladies Only."

So Poo-Poo and Horatio went out into the street again.

Mr. Brown used to think it was hard luck on him when he had to wait for his wife to buy steak. That is not half so hard as waiting for a dragon to come out of a beauty parlor.

Horatio and Poo-Poo went back to the automobile, and soon Mrs. Brown came with the parcels, and Mr. Brown came, very cross, as he always was after he had had his hair cut. And they sat and waited till Ermyntrude came walking very delicately along the road to them, and Mr. Brown suddenly said: —

"My golly, just look at that!"

Mᵐᵉ Yvonne
de Paradis
Salon
de Beauté

They almost didn't recognize Ermyntrude. She had had her eyebrows plucked into arches, and there was black stuff on her eyelashes, and red stuff on her mouth, and she was smiling a very delicate smile, so as to show it off, and each step she took she lifted her feet high so that everybody could see the polish on her claws, and long before she reached the car, they could smell all the things that had been put on her.

"My golly," said Mr. Brown again, "I think it's perfectly dreadful!"

"It's nothing of the sort," said Mrs. Brown indignantly. "It's only natural."

"Natural?" said Mr. Brown. "That's the last thing I'd call it."

"I mean it's only natural that Ermyntrude should want to look pretty," said Mrs. Brown. "After all, she's growing up. Most young people want to look like movie stars."

"And now I come to think of it," said Mr. Brown, "there are several movie stars who look just like Ermyntrude."

"You men are all alike," said Mrs. Brown.

"And you women would call black white, just to defend each other," said Mr. Brown. By this time Ermyntrude had come as far as the big plate-glass windows of Mr. Cholmondeley's Emporium, and of course she had to look at the reflection of herself as she went by the windows. So she turned to face the window, with her tail right out across the road, and she walked sideways admiring herself — and seeing how she looked with a little smile, and how she looked with a little frown, and how she looked when she walked this way, and how she looked when she walked that way. And she was so lost in looking at herself that she paid no attention to anything else, and could not realize that she was pushing back all the people along the pavement who were trying to look in the windows of the Emporium; and the tip of her tail was rattling along the row of parked cars in the same way you rattle a stick along a fence.

"It looks to me," said Mr. Brown, "as if at any moment Ermyntrude is likely to lose her popularity."

And Mrs. Brown said, "Yes, don't you think you ought to do something about it?"

"Me?" said Mr. Brown. "Oh, no! I wasn't the one who said it was perfectly natural."

And he sat back in his seat and pretended to be nearly asleep and quite indifferent.

"Poo-Poo," said Poo-Poo's mother, "run quick and make Ermyntrude come along at once."

So Poo-Poo ran and wriggled through the crowd that was piling up beside Ermyntrude, and he said to her: —

"Come along, you silly old thing."

And Ermyntrude looked round at him with her eyebrows arched, and then looked away again in a very superior fashion, because she would not pay any attention to little grubby boys who called her a "silly old thing."

And Poo-Poo stamped his feet (and it's a very long time

since I asked you what Poo-Poo's other name was) and said: "COME ALONG AT ONCE," the way his mother spoke to him sometimes.

And Ermyntrude looked at him again, and looked away again in a way that would have made Poo-Poo feel very small indeed if he had stopped to think about it. And Poo-Poo would have been angry except that he was so anxious to get Ermyntrude away that he didn't have time to stop and think about being angry.

He had a very good idea, and so he made himself smile in a superior fashion, just like Ermyntrude, and he made a little bow, and he held out his arm, and he said in a very superior voice: —

"Would your ladyship be so good as to be so kind as to be so gracious as to accompany your humble servant on a short promenade along this very inferior street?"

And Ermyntrude smiled very graciously and put her hand through Poo-Poo's arm and walked along with him through the crowd, and she nodded and smiled very graciously to the people on each side.

They came up to the automobile, and Mrs. Brown said, "Now run along home, Ermyntrude, with Horatio, like a good dragon."

And Ermyntrude still looked very superior until Mr. Brown suddenly leant forward and said: —

"I'm going to count five, Ermyntrude, and if you aren't running home like a good dragon by the time I get to five, I will call up every Dalmatian dog within a radius of fifty miles, and they will all come and nip your tail. One, two, THREE — " and before Mr. Brown could say "four" Ermyntrude was running up the road as if the Dalmatian dogs were already after her.

ONE DAY Mrs. Brown called: —

"Dinner's ready."

And Poo-Poo came, and his father came, but the dragons (has anyone asked you lately what the dragons' names were?) just did not come at all.

First of all, Mrs. Brown said: —

"Oh dear, those naughty dragons, they've still got to wash their hands before they have their dinner."

And then later on she said: —

"Everything's getting cold. I do wish those dragons would hurry up."

And then she went to the window, and she called down into the garden, "Horatio, Ermyntrude, come along at once!"

And still the dragons did not come.

And then all of a sudden there was the most extraordinary noise in the garden that you have ever heard. It was a little like a railway engine whistle with a touch of violin, as though someone were playing the bagpipes on a barrel organ. It really was a very extraordinary noise. Sometimes it reminded you of forty thousand china dishes all tumbling down a chute at once, and at other times it sounded as if the biggest knife you've ever seen were scraping the biggest tin plate you've ever come across.

Mr. Brown put down his knife and fork, and he said: —

"That just settles it. I've had enough of dragons to last me two million years, to say nothing of little boys."

And Mrs. Brown said, "Something's happened to them."

And Poo-Poo did not say anything at all, because when he heard the noise he ran out of the dining room very fast to see what was the matter.

Out in the garden Ermyntrude was lying in a coil, and Horatio was walking up and down looking very pleased with himself. And as he walked up and down he opened his mouth and made noises as if a million lawn-mowers which had not been oiled since the Declaration of Independence were being pushed very fast over a mile of pebble beach to the music of a lot of circus organs all playing different tunes accompanied by the sound of all the steam riveters in every shipyard between here and the Sea of Okhotsk. Poo-Poo thought it was simply grand (so that I do not think that it is necessary for you to look in the Atlas to find where the Sea of Okhotsk is).

And Poo-Poo started to run to Ermyntrude to see what had happened, and Horatio got in his way as he marched up and down. Poo-Poo tried to step round him, but Horatio still got in his way.

"Come out of my way, you stupid old thing," said Poo-Poo.

But whichever way he walked, there was Horatio in front of him. So Poo-Poo started to run, but so did Horatio; and still, wherever Poo-Poo went, there was Horatio in his way; even though Horatio did not leave off singing his song, and even though he was dodging about, he managed to walk very triumphantly, stepping high with his tail in the air.

Then Mr. Brown came out into the garden looking very cross.

"Horatio," he said, "you're making more noise than a tame duck!"

"He won't let me go by, Father," said Poo-Poo. "I tell you what, I'll run round one end of him, and you run round the other."

So Mr. Brown ran round Horatio's tail, while Poo-Poo ran round Horatio's head. And of course Mr. Brown was able to get by, but had no sooner done that, than up got Ermyntrude; and whichever way Mr. Brown went, there was Ermyntrude in the way. Mr. Brown ran one way, and Ermyntrude ran that way; and Mr. Brown ran the other way, and Ermyntrude ran that way. And Poo-Poo ran one way, and Horatio ran that way; and Poo-Poo ran the other way, and Horatio ran that way. And Mr. Brown said: —

"I'm thoroughly tired of this."

And then Mrs. Brown came into the garden.

"Whatever do you think you're doing?" she said to the four of them. "I've never seen anything so silly in all my life, and as for the noise . . . !"

"Thank goodness you've come, my dear," said Mr. Brown, still running up and down with Ermyntrude running up and down in front of him. "I've never been beaten by a dragon in my life, and I'm not going to start now. Please, my dear, run round to the other side of the garden quick and see what's going on there."

So Mrs. Brown dodged Poo-Poo and Mr. Brown and the two dragons, and ran around the edge of the garden as fast as she could. Horatio wanted very much to stop her, but if he stopped her it meant that he'd let Poo-Poo go by. I do not know whether you've ever seen a dragon want to come in half, but Horatio would gladly have come in half if he could have at that moment. But he had to stay in one piece, and so Mrs. Brown was able to run round him into the far corner of the garden. And as she did so, Horatio left off his noise, and the silence was so deafening in comparison that it was as if a million cannons were going off.

And Mrs. Brown stood and looked at what she saw there, and she looked and she looked, and at last she said very loudly: —

"Why, it's an egg."

And although Horatio was very worried, because he was afraid Mrs. Brown might do the egg some damage, he still walked about very proudly, and so did Ermyntrude — stepping very high with their tails waving and a proud smile on their faces. And after a moment or two, Horatio opened his mouth and was just going to start making his noise again, when Poo-Poo's father said: —

"Horatio, please don't. I just couldn't bear any more of it."

And Horatio shut his mouth and tried to make up for the absence of noise by dancing along the edge of the lawn. A dragon dancing is a very remarkable sight indeed, and when Ermyntrude joined him and they did it together, it was not like anything even Mr. Brown (who was a very clever man) had ever imagined in all his whole life.

"What sort of egg is it?" called Poo-Poo to Mrs. Brown.

"Well, it's shaped like an egg," said Mrs. Brown.

"How big is it?" asked Poo-Poo.

"Is it about this long and that wide — something between a concertina and a moving van?" asked Mr. Brown.

"That's right," said Mrs. Brown.

119

"Well, that's a pretty fair average dragon's egg," said Mr. Brown.

And Mrs. Brown said, "What clever dragons you are!" to Horatio and Ermyntrude.

"I want to see," said Poo-Poo. And he was dancing about with excitement nearly as much as the two dragons were. "Please, Horatio, let me come by. Please — I won't do anything to your egg — really I won't."

So Horatio let Poo-Poo come by, and Ermyntrude let Mr. Brown come by, and they walked up and looked at the egg from a short distance, while Horatio and Ermyntrude stood and looked on, still a little anxious.

"My goodness me," said Mrs. Brown suddenly, "that egg is hot."

And when they held their hands out to it, it warmed them the way a fire does.

"Of course it's hot," said Mr. Brown (what do you remember about him?). "All dragons' eggs are hot. They won't hatch if they're not."

And he had no sooner said this than Horatio stretched himself out on the ground with his nose pointing at the egg, and he breathed in and out very deeply, and faster and faster, and first a little flame came out of his mouth, and as he went on breathing, the flame grew larger and larger and fiercer and fiercer until it played on the egg, and there was a big rush of sparks like the

most magnificent fireworks you have ever seen. And Horatio
blew and blew, and the flame played more and more fiercely
round the egg until it was glowing like a bit of the sunset, or
like a very large tomato with a lamp inside. Only then did
Horatio leave off blowing and allow the flame to die away, while
the egg lay there glowing.

"Are you sure that's good for the egg?" asked Mrs. Brown.

"Of course," said Mr. Brown. "Dragons' eggs won't hatch unless that is done to them, my dear."

"Well then," asked Mrs. Brown, "how would you set about cooking a dragon's egg, if you wanted to cook one?"

"Well, then you have to do the opposite thing," explained Mr. Brown. "You put it in ice-water three-and-a-half minutes if you want it soft-boiled, and five minutes if you want it hard. And they are very good either way, with pepper and salt and a bit of butter."

He was so busy explaining this to Mrs. Brown, that he forgot all about Horatio, who had heard what he said, and came walking up to him looking very fierce indeed, with his tail as stiff as a poker.

"That's all right, Horatio," said Mr. Brown hastily, "we wouldn't dream of doing that to your egg."

"Of course not," said Mrs. Brown indignantly.

"Of course not," said Poo-Poo.

So they stood and looked at the egg a little while longer, and then of course Poo-Poo's mother began to think practical things as she always did, and she said: —

"All this time the dinner's getting cold. COME ALONG, ALL OF YOU."

When Mrs. Brown spoke like that, Mr. Brown and Poo-Poo always knew that they had better do what they were told, and they started going back to the house. And Horatio followed after them a little reluctantly — looking back at Ermyntrude, who was keeping guard over the egg.

And so they ate their dinner, with Horatio running backwards and forwards with choice pieces to Ermyntrude. And when dinner was finished, Poo-Poo spent the rest of the time until it was dark and bedtime watching Horatio heat up the egg at regular intervals. Then Mrs. Brown took Poo-Poo upstairs to go to bed, but Poo-Poo had hardly undone the first button before there came a tremendous knock, knock, knock, on the front door. And Mrs. Brown ran down to open it, and of course Poo-Poo ran down to see who it was, and Mr. Brown came along grumbling and saying: —

"What with dragons' eggs and knocks on the door, a man doesn't have a minute's peace."

And when they opened the door, there were some firemen with their helmets and their uniforms standing grouped round the door.

RL

"Good evening, MR. KIRKPATRICK," said Mr. Brown to the chief fireman (his first name was HEZEKIAH).

"Good evening, Mr. Brown," said Mr. Kirkpatrick. "Would you mind calling off your dragon?"

"Calling off my dragon?" said Mr. Brown.

"Calling off your dragon," said Mr. Kirkpatrick.

"Calling off . . . ?" said Mr. Brown.

"That's what I said," said Mr. Kirkpatrick.

"What have I got to call him off from?" asked Mr. Brown.

"He's interfering with us in the execution of our duty," said Mr. Kirkpatrick. "At least he would interfere with us if we started to execute our duty, as anyone can see with half an eye, so that we haven't dared start."

"Really, Mr. Kirkpatrick," said Mr. Brown, "this may all be very plain to you, but I really do not understand what you're talking about, and I do not think it can be my fault, because I have the reputation for being — " (We all know what Mr. Brown had the reputation for being, so we do not have to finish what he said.)

"Well, come and see," said Mr. Kirkpatrick.

So they walked along the front of the house, and there were the fire engines and the ladders, and dozens of firemen in their helmets. And there was a hose lying across the street with two men all ready to work it. And standing in front of them was Horatio with his teeth exposed and his tail all stiff and looking much fiercer even than he did when Mr. Brown was talking about cooking dragons' eggs.

"If we were to turn on that hose," said Mr. Kirkpatrick, "that dragon would go for us, or my name's not — " (We know what his name was, so we do not have to finish his sentence for him either.)

"But what do you want to turn the hose on for?" asked Poo-Poo.

"Because there's a fire," said Mr. Kirkpatrick.

"A fire?" asked Mr. Brown.

"There's the fire," said Mr. Kirkpatrick, pointing down the garden to where the dragon's egg glowed like a tomato with an arc lamp inside.

"Sometimes it's much worse than that," went on Mr. Kirkpatrick.

Horatio soon showed Poo-Poo and Mr. Brown what they were talking about, because now that they had come out and could keep their eye on the fireman on the hose, Horatio scuttled back to the egg and started blowing up his flame upon it, and there was a big rush of sparks like the finest firework anyone had seen, and it showed up especially brilliantly in the darkness.

"There, you see?" said Mr. Kirkpatrick.

"I would have to be completely blind, not merely short-sighted, not to see that," said Mr. Brown. "But at the same time — please do not think that I have any intention of being rude —

I fail to see what business it is of yours, even though if anybody could see that, it would be me, because, as you know, I am a very clever man."

"It's our duty to put out fires," said Mr. Kirkpatrick.

And by this time Mrs. Brown was tired of having the two men argue with each other.

"My goodness gracious me," said Mrs. Brown. "Can't a poor innocent dragon even lay an egg without all the firemen in the town wanting to come and squirt hoses on it?"

"We didn't even know the dragon had laid an egg," said the chief fireman (what was his name?).

"It only happens once in a million years," explained Mr. Brown, "and that's not a bad thing either, because otherwise we would be having dragons all over the place."

"Well, if that's all it is," said Mr. Kirkpatrick, "we had better go home again. And as for you, Mr. Brown, it would have saved a good deal of time, in the first place, if you had explained what was happening instead of merely saying back to me what I said to you."

"I thought I was following a very good example," said Mr. Brown. "Anyway, good evening, gentlemen. And don't leave too many ladders or fire engines lying about when you clear up. Firemen and little boys are all alike."

OF COURSE, what Poo-Poo wanted to know more than anything else was how soon it would be before the baby dragon
hatched out of the egg, but even his father could not tell him
for sure.

"You see," he said, "it depends on a great many circumstances. One of the things we don't know is whether the new
dragon is going to be left-handed or not, because of course
if he's left-handed it will naturally take longer, that stands to
reason, and the latitude and the longitude, and the altitude,
and the barometer readings, all have to be taken into account."

"Why?" asked Poo-Poo.

"Because you have to make corrections to Greenwich Time.

And that's not all. It depends partly on whether it's Tuesday or Wednesday. So you see, it's very hard to be quite accurate, but I can tell you this, if it isn't next week, it will be some other time."

"I see," said Poo-Poo, because he was always a very polite boy, "but why I wanted to know is because of the baby dragon's birthday party."

"Birthday?" said Mr. Brown, very surprised.

"Poo-Poo's been talking about this birthday party ever since the day before yesterday," said Poo-Poo's mother.

"So you think a dragon's birthday is the day he comes out of the egg?"

"Yes, of course," said Poo-Poo.

"Well, some people would say it's the day the egg is laid," said Mr. Brown. "So that you're a bit late."

"I don't think so," said Poo-Poo.

"Well, there's another thing," said Mr. Brown. "When that dragon comes out of the egg, he will be only just beginning, won't he? He won't be one or two or three, he'll be naught or zero. I really don't see how you can have a naughth birthday."

"Oh," said Poo-Poo, rather disappointed. He had not thought of that.

"When you're ten," went on Mr. Brown, "you have a cake with ten candles on it. Don't you think it would be silly to have a cake with no candles on it?"

Well, that was where Mr. Brown was wrong, because Poo-

Poo knew that a cake was a cake, whether it had ten candles on it or no candles on it, and he started to say so.

"It's like this," said Mrs. Brown (and as soon as Poo-Poo heard Mrs. Brown speaking on his side, he knew that there would be a birthday party), "after all, when you're nine you have one cake with nine candles, and when you're ten, you have one cake with ten candles, so that when you're naught, you have one cake and no candles. Your age doesn't affect the cake, it only affects the candles."

"*Umph!*" said Mr. Brown, because it was not very often that he lost an argument (I expect you can tell me why). "First it's little boys, and then it's dragons, and then it's birthday parties, and what with one thing and another a man can't have a moment's peace in his own house," he said, very bitterly indeed; so that Poo-Poo laughed, because Poo-Poo always did laugh when his father spoke bitterly, and then he went away to write the invitations for the party.

Of course Mrs. Brown tried to help him, and at first it was easy enough. They started off by writing: —

Mr. and Mrs. Horatio Heavyside Dragon [can you guess who Mrs. Horatio Heavyside Dragon was?] *would like you to come to a party to celebrate the naughth birthday of their . . .*

That was where they were stuck for a moment, because they didn't know whether to put son or daughter, but very often Mrs. Brown was just as clever as Mr. Brown (in fact oftener,

129

but she did not call so much attention to it) and so she suggested that they say "child."

Mr. and Mrs. Horatio Heavyside Dragon would like you to come to a party to celebrate the naughth birthday of their child . . .

And there they were stuck again, because they ought to have put the child's name here, and they had no idea at all what the name was going to be.

"I think we'd better leave the child's name out," said Poo-Poo. And so they did.

But then the next question was what date they should put on the invitation. And there they were stuck once more.

"I don't think Father said what date it was going to be," said Poo-Poo.

"I don't think he did," said Mrs. Brown. "He said a lot of other things the way he always does, but he didn't say that."

"Well, I'm going to ask him again," said Poo-Poo. And so he did.

And Mr. Brown thought very deeply for a little while.

"Are you going to write the invitations yourself?" asked Mr. Brown.

"Yes, of course," said Poo-Poo.

"Well, that's easy," said Mr. Brown. "I've never known you to write anything yet without making a blot. Write and say, 'on the blot*th* of this month' so that you leave a blot where the date ought to be. And then I expect they will telephone to you and ask you what the number was you meant to put where you put the blot, and then you can say, 'On Dragons' Day, of course,' very indignantly, and perhaps they will think they ought to know when Dragons' Day is and won't like to ask you any more questions."

"But do you think Mother would like me to do that?" asked Poo-Poo doubtfully. "She might say it isn't the proper thing to do, especially as I don't know when Dragons' Day is."

"Oh that's all right," said Mr. Brown. "There never has been a Dragons' Day so far, and the day that egg hatches will be the first Dragons' Day, and so there's no reason at all why you shouldn't say so."

"I see," said Poo-Poo.

"But now we've got it all settled," said Mr. Brown, "if I were you (I don't think I am, but supposing I were) — if I were you, now that we've got all this settled, I shouldn't do anything of the kind."

"Why not?" asked Poo-Poo.

"Well," said Mr. Brown, "there are one hundred and seventeen reasons which I can think of at present, and I expect while I was telling them to you I could think of seventy-one more, and while I was telling you those, I could think of forty-three more, and while I was telling you those, I could think of thirty-seven more, and while I was telling you those — well, anyway, you can see it would be a long time before I got down to the last reason."

"But what's the first reason?" asked Poo-Poo.

"The first reason," said Mr. Brown, "is because it isn't respectable or good or right or proper for a little boy to do things like that. That's the first reason, and the second reason is that you will not find it necessary to send out any invitations."

"Why not?" asked Poo-Poo.

"Didn't you know I was a very clever man?" asked Mr. Brown. (Did you know that?) "Here I am telling you something and you say, 'Why?' 'Why?' 'Why?'"

"I didn't," said Poo-Poo. "I said, 'Why not?'"

"I feel," said Mr. Brown suddenly, "that if I hear one more word from you in the next hour and three quarters, something terrible will happen. Either I shall have a fit, or you will be spanked, and I am quite sure you would not like either of those to happen."

"I wouldn't like to be spanked," said Poo-Poo.

"Then run away as fast as you can," said Mr. Brown, "run away or else —— " But by the time Mr. Brown had said the word "or," and before he had said the word "else," Poo-Poo had run away (although he was still wondering why it wouldn't be necessary to send out the invitations).

And as you will see as you go on reading this book, quite a lot of things happened before he knew.

DO YOU REMEMBER how whenever Horatio blew flames over the egg, there was a big rush of sparks up into the air? Of course those sparks came from the eggshell, which meant that whenever Horatio warmed up the egg, he not merely warmed it up, but burnt a little of the shell away, so that the shell grew thinner and thinner. In fact, it was not very long before the shell grew quite transparent, and when you looked through it you could see the baby dragon inside. It was rather like one of those glass balls that you use for paper weights, with a snowstorm inside, and a little figure. The figure was the baby dragon, and the snowstorm was all the other things that you find inside dragons' eggs. In fact, if a baby dragon ever wants to be naughty, the time for him to do that is when the eggshell becomes transparent, because then everybody can see him being naughty even though his father and mother cannot get at him to punish him. The only trouble is that when you are inside an eggshell it is not easy to be really naughty, as of course you know, if ever you've been inside an eggshell.

The first time Poo-Poo peeped into the egg and saw the baby dragon inside, he ran and fetched his father and mother so that they could see as well. Mr. Brown peeped into the egg first this side and then that side.

"So *that* is MAXIMILIAN," he said, because of course, being a very clever man, he knew right away what the baby dragon's name was.

And Ermyntrude wagged her tail because of all her maternal instincts, and Horatio smiled and blew flames all over the egg until it glowed like the sunset, and Maximilian inside waved and grinned at them.

So Poo-Poo used to take his toys down to the egg, and play with them so that Maximilian could see him. But then one day he had his electric train there, and Mr. Brown ran the lawn mower over the electric wire from the house and broke the wire and spoiled the lawn mower and blew all the fuses in the house, and was just as angry with Poo-Poo as if it had been Poo-Poo's fault.

It took a very long time to get the house straight again after that, so that it was just as well that the egg was red-hot, because Mrs. Brown found it very useful to cook pancakes and bacon on; although that was very hard luck on Maximilian, who used to see pancakes sizzling away just over his nose while he simply could not get at them at all. They made his mouth water so much that in the end Mrs. Brown had to leave off cooking pancakes on the egg in case Maximilian's mouth-watering should make the shell crack before it was supposed to.

And all the time the eggshell grew thinner and thinner, and more and more transparent every time Horatio heated it up, until at last it was just like a bubble which had the loveliest colors playing over it whenever it was thoroughly hot.

And then at last, Horatio started to blow on it, and the sparks rushed up, and then suddenly the bubble was not there any longer. It had just disappeared, burnt away entirely — which is the explanation of why you never see any dragons' eggs in the museum. And there was Maximilian standing on the grass, looking a little puzzled at first, now that he was out of his egg. But

of course that did not last very long, because in two-and-three-quarters seconds he started scampering about the grass and wagging his tail, the way he had seen his father and mother do, and trying to act just like a grown-up dragon, because of course he had never seen any baby dragons to imitate.

And now that Maximilian was out of the egg, something happened which showed that Mr. Brown was a very clever man, which I think you have already suspected. Because the very day it happened, all the newspapers came out with great big headlines: *THE LITTLE STRANGER ARRIVES, WELCOME TO MAXIMILIAN H. DRAGON, WELL DONE ERMYNTRUDE!* — although the last one was not really fair, because it was Horatio who had done all the work in keeping the egg warm.

And of course, the moment the newspapers appeared, everybody who knew Horatio and Ermyntrude wanted to congratulate them; and so, just as Mr. Brown had predicted, there was no need to send out the invitations at all. Because Poo-Poo had only to ask the people when he saw them.

First of all, MR. MAXWELL MURRAY McINTOSH came, and he brought a nice belt made of umbrella handles (so perhaps you can guess now who Maxwell Murray McIntosh was), and MISS AMELIA MONTGOMERY brought some complimentary tickets for the theater (so that you can guess who *she* was), and ARAMINTA WIGGINS came, but didn't bring any

136

present at all (so that perhaps you can guess who *she* was). And PATRICK MACGILLICUDDY brought a fine silver star (so that you can guess who *he* was); and MISS MELISANDE WINTERGREEN brought a Certificate of Good Conduct (she said that if Maximilian didn't have that as soon as he was born he probably never would have one at all, so that perhaps you can guess who *she* was). And MR. HERBERT JEREMIAH O'SHAUGHNESSY brought a box of alphabet blocks, so that you can guess who *he* was, and MR. JAMES PONSONBY AUCHINLECK brought a crateful of watermelons (so that you can guess who *he* was); and MR. QUENTIN FAZACKELY (Mrs. Fazackely used to call him Q) brought a quart of ice cream (so that you know who *he* was), and MR. PERCIVAL COROMANDEL brought them a perpetual free pass to Coromandel's Great Three-Ring Circus (that makes it very easy for you), and MR. GIULIO FANTOCHINI (that's one you've forgotten) sent a phonograph record of his beautiful voice, and DR. PACKINGHAMPTON said he would save up his present until the next story, so that you will have to wait a little while before you will know what he gave Maximilian.

And MISS FLUFFKIN SKINILIMBS gave a picture of herself standing on the back of a horse, which was convenient because then they could remember who she was (the same as you), and ALOYSIUS PENNEFATHER brought him a little model Dalmatian dog, and MR. SEBASTIAN FITZALLAN brought Maximilian the Freedom of the City in a little tin case, and GEORGE FABRICIUS MARTINELLI brought him a toy motor horn.

MRS. THEODOSIA DEVEREUX sent a baby carriage and MARMADUKE PRENDERGAST DEVEREUX sent a rattle, and CAPTAIN WELLINGTON SIMPKINS and MR. AGAMEMNON FEATHERSTONE brought him a ship, of course (I expect you could have guessed that without my telling you, because of course you know who they were). And MADAME YVONNE DE PARADIS sent a manicure set for Ermyntrude, because she could not think of anything to give to Maximilian.

MR. HEZEKIAH KIRKPATRICK brought a real fireman's helmet, which was a little too big for Maximilian at present.

And that settles all Poo-Poo's friends except for Dr. Packinghampton, and you will soon know what he gave.

·17·

SO THEY WERE GOING to have the party that night, and of course everybody was very much excited; even Mr. Brown was excited, so that it quite slipped out of his mind to warn them about keeping an eye on Maximilian because Maximilian was very new to the world, and had had no experience of it at present. (At least Mr. Brown always said that he would have warned them if he had thought of it.)

Everybody was busy getting ready for the party. Mrs. Brown was cooking like anything, and Horatio and Poo-Poo were running about with chairs.

Ermyntrude was doing so many things that when she fell

over Maximilian she said, "Get out of my way, do!" as if Maximilian had been her child for several years instead of just for an hour or two, and as if she had no maternal instincts at all.

And Mr. Brown was going from room to room trying to find a little peace and quiet, and not finding any.

So when Ermyntrude told Maximilian to get out of her way, he got out of her way by going into the street and looking for adventures in the great big world — about which he knew nothing, as Mr. Brown ought to have told them.

Maximilian went along one street and he went along another street, and he liked everything he saw, and after a little while he came to a big hole in the side of a hill. Maximilian stopped and looked at the hole for a long time. And he thought to himself that if this were a mouse hole, or even a rabbit hole, it must be the home of the finest mouse or rabbit that the world had ever seen. He did not know what the long bars of iron were that ran up into the hill and disappeared into the darkness in one direction, and disappeared into the far distance in the other direction, but he didn't pay much attention to them. He sat down close to the hill waiting for the mouse or rabbit to come out, because then he thought that would be another very nice contribution to make to the party. And he sat and he waited and he waited and waited, and after a long time he heard a noise far down the tunnel, and he crouched all ready to spring, and the noise came nearer and nearer until at last whatever it was came rushing out of the tunnel very fast indeed, but not too fast for Maximilian, because he was ready for it, and he made one spring, and he pounced upon the rabbit or the mouse or whatever-it-was (I expect you know what it was) as it came rushing out of the tunnel. The whatever-it-was did not pay any attention to Maximilian at all. One moment Maximilian jumped, and the next moment there he was lying by the railway, and the thing he had jumped at was quite a long way away, and he had to pick himself up and find his way home again.

Back at home all the guests had arrived: Mr. Maxwell Murray McIntosh, and Miss Amelia Montgomery, and Miss Araminta Wiggins, and Patrick Macgillicuddy, and Miss Melisande Wintergreen, and Mr. Herbert Jeremiah O'Shaughnessy, and Mr. James Ponsonby Auchinleck, and Mr. Quentin Fazackely, and Mr. Percival Coromandel, and Mr. Giulio Fantochini, and Miss Fluffkin Skinilimbs, and Aloysius Pennefather, and Mr. Sebastian Fitzallan, and George Fabricius Martinelli. There were Mrs. Theodosia Devereux, and Marmaduke Prendergast Devereux, and Captain Wellington Simpkins and Mr. Agamemnon Featherstone, and Madame Yvonne de Paradis, and Mr. Hezekiah Kirkpatrick.

And last of all came Dr. Packinghampton, and he had not brought a present for Maximilian.

They had looked around for the young dragon that the party

was about, and he was not there. And Mrs. Brown was very cross, and Horatio went round stamping his feet, and Ermyntrude lashed her tail, all of which made it look as if something serious would happen to Maximilian when he came home.

And Mr. Brown was saying, "Once a man gets dragons into his house, he never has a moment's peace."

And after waiting a little while longer, they all started getting worried instead of getting angry, and began to wonder what had happened to Maximilian and to discuss what they ought to do.

And Mr. Brown went round saying, "I'm thoroughly tired of dragons. I shall really have to do something about it."

And then just at the last minute, in walked Maximilian. And he was scraped and he was scratched, and he was cut and he was bruised, and he was dirty and he was untidy, and altogether he looked as if something had happened to him. And of course, everybody forgot to be angry, and Mrs. Brown and Ermyntrude and Miss Amelia Montgomery and Miss Araminta Wiggins and Miss Melisande Wintergreen and Mrs. Theodosia Devereux all rushed up to him and said: —

"Poor little Maximilian, whatever has happened to you?"

And Maximilian could not tell them. He could just stand there untidy and dirty and bruised and cut and scratched and scraped.

"Oh dear oh dear oh dear," said Mrs. Brown.

But Dr. Packinghampton was there, and he had not brought

a present. So he opened his bag, and he got out sticking plaster and bandages and ointment and iodine and cotton and all the other things, and he bandaged up Maximilian's wounds instead of giving him a present.

And when that was done, the party was ready to start, and that is the last story about Poo-Poo and the dragons.